P's
3 WOMEN

Originally published in Portuguese as *Tres Mulheres De Tres Pppes* by Perspectiva, São Paulo, 1977, and in English as *P's Three Women* by Avon Bard, 1984
Copyright © 1977 by Paulo Emílio Sales Gomes
Translation copyright © 1984 by Margaret A. Neves
Foreword © 2012 by Margaret A. Neves
First Dalkey Archive edition, 2012

Library of Congress Cataloging-in-Publication Data

Gomes, Paulo Emílio Salles, 1916-1977.
  [Três mulheres de três PPPês. English]
  P's three women / Paulo Emílio Sales Gomes ; translated and foreword by Margaret A. Neves. -- 1st Dalkey Archive ed.
    p. cm.
  "Originally published in Portuguese as Tres Mulheres De Tres Pppes by Perspectiva, São Paulo, 1977, and in English as P's Three Women by Avon Bard, 1984"--T.p. verso.
  ISBN 978-1-56478-738-5 (pbk. : acid-free paper)
  I. Neves, Margaret A. II. Title.
  PQ9698.17.O446T713 2012
  869.3'42--dc23
                    2012013730

Partially funded by a grant from the Illinois Arts Council, a state agency

MINISTÉRIO DA CULTURA
Fundação BIBLIOTECA NACIONAL

Obra publicada com o apoio do Ministério da Cultura do Brasil/ Fundação Biblioteca Nacional/ Coordenadoria Geral do Livro e da Leitura.

Work published with the support of Brazil's Ministry of Culture / National Library Foundation / Coordinator General of the Book and Reading.

www.dalkeyarchive.com

Cover: design and composition by Sarah French, illustration by Nick Motte

P's
3 WOMEN

PAULO EMÍLIO SALES GOMES
TRANSLATED BY
MARGARET A. NEVES

DALKEY ARCHIVE PRESS
CHAMPAIGN / DUBLIN / LONDON

Translator's Foreword

Translating, for all its recognized dangers, is a highly rewarding endeavor. It involves making the edges of different realities fit smoothly together and rendering another person's thought process both intelligible and palatable. The literary translator needs the full arsenal of any wordsmith—imagery, sound, metaphor, colloquialism, and so on—but must never lose fidelity to the original author's artistic intent. Though the responsibility is serious, the translation process has always been, for me, a source of deep gratification, fascination, and fun. Brazilian literature is a treasure trove.

The book you have before you is one of my favorites. Polished in many-faceted planes, it glitters like a small gem. Though at first sight *P's Three Women* appears to be merely a farcical exposé of conjugal mismatch, a Thurberesque war-between-the-sexes charade, we are soon given hints that the author has deeper intentions.

A wealthy, fiftyish man in the São Paulo of the early 1970s whose interests (besides women) include politics and military strategy, P belongs to Brazil's most elite and privileged class. He lives in a highly exclusive old-money neighborhood. This context—this specific time, place, and society—may seem unimportant, but in fact it is a quite cleverly placed backdrop for the foibles of a character who is something of a stereotype. As a narrator, P is highly unreliable: he would have us believe that deep down he is a liberal and "anti-family," when in fact he gets on well with his brothers and his liberality does not go beyond his support for orthographic reforms. He has deep admiration for various iconic pillars of *Paulistano** life and history, and actually resents real changes to the social order.

We are struck immediately by P's precise, almost stilted prose narration, a device reinforcing the pomposity of his character and at the same time highlighting the theme of communication. P has a deep respect for language, and goes so far as to extol its articulate use by two of his women, Helena and Her. On the other hand, the third, Ermengarda, drives him to despair with her abbreviations, nicknames, and messy style of writing. P believes in the power of words to define reality. Notice how he detests his given name and refuses to use it himself or let others do so. Ermengarda's name is "false"—it's meant to have an *H*, contrary to the orthographic rules of Brazilian Portuguese; and then Helena's son is never named at all, nor is the third woman in the novel, "Her." For someone of P's linguistic nicety, surely this namelessness is suggestive. What is not named, for P, is not completely real—hence his inability to see what is before his eyes, much less come to terms with his own emotionally stunted identity. Real communication, for P, happens only in a few sharp flashes in the story, and it is always painful.

Paulo Emílio Sales Gomes was well known as a film critic, and his knowledge of cinematic technique serves him well as a novelist. It is evident in the plot twists, timing of events, and even in visual and auditory details such as the picture of the girl with the turkey, or Ermengarda's demand, during sex, to hear her name

---

* The term *Paulistano* refers to someone from the city of São Paulo. *Paulista* means someone from the state of the same name.

pronounced with an aspirated *H*. Perception, deception, misconception—all are masterfully employed with varying degrees of focus and luminosity, as if a camera lens were showing us where and how to see things. And all this without direct dialogue between characters—P narrates throughout. In each of the chapters we are taken through the same schematic pattern: first, the version of events according to P, in which his vanity and obtuseness dominate. After a suspenseful crescendo, the same events are revealed to him (and us) in a completely different light through the prism of the woman's understanding. At each of these points, P has what might be termed a revelation of truth, a shift from the inauthentic to the authentic. Yet each time he fails to move beyond the limits of tragicomic absurdity.

If we accept that P can be taken as part stereotype, the novel gains in depth. São Paulo in the early 1970s was expanding its already notable economic and political importance, and well-connected families like P's were growing ever wealthier. Respectability, tradition, and right-wing power were defining qualities for people of P's sort, along with a heavy dose of corruption. (Note the bribes to the Paraguayan consul—divorce was then illegal in Brazil.) The country was only just emerging from dictatorship, and political repression, though quieter than in some Latin American countries, was very real. In all three segments of *P's Three Women*, seemingly casual references to police brutality occur. Paulo Emílio Sales Gomes is parodying the *Paulistano* elite of his generation who made no effort to shake off the old-boy paralysis of their society and indeed contributed to its oppressiveness and stratification, through self-deception and by default.

However, that is not to say that this novel is primarily political in intent. Although himself an activist, notably in São Paulo's uprising in 1935 against the regime of Getúlio Vargas, the author has not set out to present a manifesto. Rather, he is inviting us to contrast appearances with reality, convention with sincerity, lust with genuine love, and thereby gain insight. For beneath the narrator's Jamesian prose and *Paulistano* snobbery, P is nevertheless a figure of a certain pathos. The reader cannot help feeling sorry for him, even while laughing at his antics. He really does have perfect manners, and they hobble his life. He tries to find love, despite his blind self-centeredness, and fails. He writes a pretentious "Eulogy to the São Paulo Lady," and at the end of his life turns in crazed despair to numerology for existential aid. The author wants us to laugh at him, but he also wants us to see P's sad futility as emblematic of his species, and be instructed.

The reader is left wishing that Paulo Emílio Sales Gomes had written more novels. His major focus was on cinema. In 1965 he created the first Brazilian course in filmmaking at the University of Brasilia. This activity, viewed as potentially subversive by the government then holding power, was unfortunately terminated. In 1968, however, he returned to teaching, this time History of Brazilian Cinema at the University of São Paulo. Born in 1916, as a young man Sales Gomes was drawn, along with many intellectuals of the time, to communism as a political and social ideal. He later tempered his views, declaring, "As happens with other loves, I believe I was enriched by communism. At any rate, I think I escaped a greater danger, that of abandoning communism only to bog down in anti-communism." (*Criticas no Suplemento Literario,* vol. II) He worked both independently and in collaboration with others on screenplays, books, criticism, and commentary. He was married to the well-known novelist and short-story writer Lygia Fagundes Telles, who co-authored a screenplay with him based on Machado de Assis's classic novel *Dom Casmurro*. Sales Gomes's best-known book is a study of the life and work of the French filmmaker Jean Vigo.

A couple of notes on the translation. In Portuguese, the title of this book is *Três Mulheres de três PPPês*. The expression "p-p-p" means chitchat, bla-bla-bla. Hence, three women and their chitchats. In addition to echoing the narrator's first initial, the term is lightly condescending to the women, just like P himself

There is also the question of Dr. Bulhões's name, which is a normal Portuguese surname, but when a *C* is substituted for its *B*, it becomes *culhões,* a vulgar term for testicles. In English, it simply wasn't possible to bring out the subtlety of this "neighboring consonant."

My best wishes for a pleasurable read.

MARGARET A. NEVES, 2012

Twice with Helena

IF it hadn't been for my arthritis I would never have met Helena again. I realize it's inappropriate to begin a story of youth by alluding to arthritis, my own or hers, but the truth is that without this malady, our meeting in São Pedro thirty years later would never have occurred. She in Pacaembu and I in Alto dos Pinheiros, each moving in different circles, taking taxis or using our own cars, neither of us frequenting nightclubs or parties and neither in the limelight, the chances of our paths crossing were negligible, and indeed for three decades they never did, as if God had answered the ardent supplications I directed heavenward. Nevertheless, if one stops to think about it, a man and a woman who are both over fifty, arthritic, affluent, and living in São Paulo, would sooner or later be bound to turn up at the same time in Águas de São Pedro, the spa village where bourgeois and middle-class rheumatics reserve rooms in two or three principal hotels.

I didn't recognize Helena at first when I saw her. She was sitting beside Professor Alberto, taking the air in the small park decorated with colorfully painted plaster

From the novel TRES MULHERES DE TRES PPPES by Paulo Emilio Salles Gomes
Translated by Margaret Abigail Neves

dwarfs. Him I recognized at once, in spite of his white hair and the modern glasses which had replaced the heavy tortoiseshell ones that used to grace his powerful nose. For years he was my mentor and close friend. The vastness of his knowledge and the way in which his intelligence could maneuver his accumulation of cultural data made me esteem the professor—when I was able to evaluate him—as the first genius I had ever met. The first and the only, I can say today as I enter old age and expect from those who are intelligent more than just multiplicity of talents. Nobody ever liked me as much as the professor did. He thought me gifted, and from grade school on he lent me books, and thus oriented my reading. His diligence continued through my university days, when I naively tried to deepen my taste for letters, art and ideas that he had determinedly aroused in me. He took upon himself the formation of my basic ideas in all areas; he met and approved my girl friends, including my first more or less professional mistress. It was he who engineered a scholarship for me to study in Europe; it was he—who never traveled—who methodically organized the itineraries and the list of indispensable visits to be made: the section of the Montparnasse Cemetery where Baudelaire is buried, the exact number of the house on rue Monsieur le Prince where Auguste Comte lived, and the address of the Vatican Library of Milan where certain lesser-known sketches of Leonardo da Vinci were kept.

To my mind of twenty, the professor's forty years made him a confirmed bachelor, and it was not without surprise that I received, in Paris, the letter announcing his marriage. During the two years that I had been abroad we had corresponded regularly, but with the passage of time I had sensed in my mentor's letters

ever-growing doses of melancholy, as well as a decline
in his fervor to cultivate me. I attributed this change in
tone to the disappointment I must be causing him. My
impartial love for culture was being replaced by a liking
for politics, a discipline he found boring. Worse yet, I
was inclined toward fascism, a movement for which
Professor Alberto had only scorn, particularly after the
appearance of integralism and the blow of the New
State. The beginning of World War II hastened my return home, and it was with a certain apprehension that I
went to meet him again, for the first time in his new
house in Pacaembu that he had taken after marrying. I
was curious to meet Helena, about whom I knew nothing more than her name, the professor's letters having
been impersonal. But she was not there; she was spending some time in Campos do Jordão, he told me with a
wide smile of welcome that I have never forgotten. For
the next few weeks he hardly let me alone. I had come
back from Europe much thinner, and this upset him
greatly; he insisted that I see several doctors and have
various laboratory tests. In spite of my excellent health I
obeyed him without resistance; I reckoned that he, like
so many others approaching old age, had become ob-
sessed with illness and was including me in his obsession. My impatience with the meticulous slowness of
the doctors disappeared upon seeing my friend's satisfaction at all the "negative" laboratory results. As for
the rest, the discussions I had feared never occurred.
When the names of Hitler or Mussolini entered the conversation—at my provocation—he would shake his head
and change the subject. One day I caught him showing
tolerance for the extremists, as we called subversives in
those days. But he disarmed me at once, explaining that
in politics, a liberal such as himself must tolerate every-

3

thing, even a fascist, although he actually tolerated only one: me.

Three weeks after my arrival, the professor left to join his wife in Campos do Jordão, inviting me to go there for a few days. I made preparations to travel with him, but the idea didn't please him. He consulted a small calendar with close attention, asked what the date was, counted on his fingers and fixed the precise moment I should arrive, three or four days hence. I then realized that he wanted to make sure that I would be at his side on my birthday, which was close, and I thanked him for remembering it. But he affected surprise, as if he only that minute remembered a date he had never let go by unrecognized.

It was easy to locate the isolated cottage, surrounded by pine trees, in Umuarama. I didn't immediately identify the girl who opened the door as Helena; I never supposed the wife of my forty-year-old friend would be so young—and above all so lovely. But a contretemps awaited me. In response to an urgent message from his family, it seemed, the professor had left that very morning, not having had time to notify me, but he would be back within four or five days. Helena announced this quickly, without looking at me, as she stood in the doorway. Her timidity was contagious. Embarrassed, I replied that it was perfectly all right, I would stay with an aunt in Capivari and would come back in a few days to see if the professor had returned. I was about to shake hands with her, when I noted a certain tremor in her lips as she walked quickly back into the house. When she finally spoke, I couldn't understand her words. From her confused stammerings I could make out only a series of negatives, pronounced with agitation.

I was perplexed and very ill at ease. Finally Helena, after a visible effort, managed to say that the professor had left explicit instructions that I install myself in the cottage and wait for his return. My constraint was as acute as hers. I resolved not to accept the situation that was being forced upon me, but Helena, controlling her nervousness, insisted that she could not let me go. She now spoke with surprising authority, though she still turned her great green eyes away from me—the only element in her behavior that had not changed since she had first opened the door. I must add that during the days I spent there, Helena never once looked at me. The first time she did so was thirty years later, in the garden with the plaster dwarfs. If I was reluctant to stay at their country house, it was because of the affliction that those shifting eyes caused me: the most beautiful eyes I had ever seen in my life, fixed always on something just to the left or right of my head. I agreed to stay only when she said that I would put her in a difficult position regarding her husband; he had insisted that I wait there for him. Much against my wishes, I took my bag to the bedroom she indicated. The cool afternoon was sunny, and with relief I accepted the suggestion that I take a solitary walk. Dinner, she told me, would be at seven.

During my walk through the woods, I couldn't stop thinking about my strange welcome. I alternately criticized and pardoned Professor Alberto, who was responsible for the uncomfortable situation. I couldn't figure out what type of woman Helena might be—what she, in her youth and beauty, could have found in the professor, an extraordinary man in so many ways, but already old and without any fortune to speak of. Nothing fit; the uncertainty of it all was disturbing. And those eyes that wouldn't meet mine!

* * *

When I went into the small dining room, Helena was waiting for me. She had dressed and combed with care, her hair piled high on her head, her long neck accentuated by a plunging décolleté gown such as one saw in American films. Her bare arms were firm and delicate. I observed that in addition to being beautiful, she was exceptionally seductive. A small fire flickered in the fireplace. She went to the kitchen various times, bringing a soup tureen, a platter with roast duck à l'orange, bottles of fine French wine. I realized, again embarrassed, that the house had no domestic employees; Helena did everything. At the same time, I took advantage of her walking back and forth to better appreciate her dress, which clung tightly to her hips. I reflected on how clothing styles had changed in my absence.

Dinner was enjoyable. In the beginning my hostess seemed stiff, but gradually her expression became more relaxed, helped perhaps by the wines, which she drank in the same quantity as I. The first time she laughed at my stories about Paris, I was dazzled. The row of fine, well-set teeth, with a tiny sliver of rosy gum visible above, constituted the final touch of desirability, and I put down my glass, suddenly feeling almost dizzy. My rapture was interrupted by a slight sensation of discomfort, and settling myself more comfortably in the chair, I perceived that I was in the midst of an erection. Perturbed, I began to talk about the professor, what he meant to me, how much I owed him, how I loved and admired him. Helena's mouth had been mobilized in the expectancy of more laughter, but it dissolved into a wan smile of approval when I mentioned her husband. Her eyes shifted from their usual point beyond me to focus on the wine bottle, which she lifted to fill our glasses to the brim. I, the recent European traveler, privately observed that to fill wineglasses to overflowing, as if one were drinking beer, was the Brazilian idea of hospitality, but I did not pursue this snobbish thought. I was dying to catch another glimpse of gum through her lovely lips, so I didn't bring up the professor again. Instead I went back to my Parisian anecdotes, with growing exaggeration and success. Several times Helena repeated her undulating trips to the kitchen. By the time I tasted the caramel pudding, the erection was no longer a bother. It was welcome. While a certain degree of drunkenness caused me ironic thoughts about the great liberal who tolerated everything, a shred of conscience pacified me with the thought that effectively I was doing nothing wrong. I offered to help Helena make the coffee and she giggled at my clumsiness. In truth, standing up, I felt clumsier than before. The undershorts and trousers of 1940 had a looseness that impeded one's either disciplining or liberating an erection. That gaze which avoided my face by moving from the top of my head to wander about the sides and lower parts of my body ran the risk of fixing itself upon a breach of manners capable of annulling the evening's enchantment. However, my scruples didn't last long; not that I overcame them, but I simply let myself be carried away on the succession of gestures, drinks, and laughter. After the coffee, Helena brought glasses and a bottle of very special champagne that I had once tasted on a visit to Reims. I was unaware that it could be purchased in Brazil, since even in Paris it was difficult to find and extremely expensive. When Helena asked me to open a second bottle, I thought about the professor's apparent increase in prosperity as I made an effort to remove the swollen cork. Helena's ever-shifting eyes had now acquired a new brilliance. It was this shine that made the idea of madness cross my mind when—after a motionless moment of silence—she resolutely advanced toward me and pressed her body against mine.

The room to which she led me was totally dark. This setting for our lovemaking remained in complete obscurity during the four days and nights that I spent with her in the cottage. Even when I sought her during full daylight, the refuge was always dark. Due to the unscheduled urgency of our desire, I spent more time in that bedroom than anywhere else in Campos do Jordão, though I never actually saw a single object, fabric, or piece of furniture it contained. Outside it, I was hardly with Helena. The *toilette* and banquet of the first night were not repeated. Discreetly dressed, she served the meals, but did not sit down at the table with me. They consisted of substantial but simple fare: rare steaks instead of duck, and pitchers of orange juice in place of wine. She authoritatively imposed the distribution of my time: when not in the darkness or at the table, I went for solitary walks through the woods or rested in my room, which she entered only to bring me eggnogs made with an excellent cognac, the consumption of which she stood watching, like a severe and efficient nurse. Indeed, the sensation that pervaded me outside our amorous moments was precisely that of one who has escaped a grave disease and is experiencing the euphoric fatigue of convalescence. The word *fatigue* is appropriate. Not that Helena was exactly insatiable, but she worked hard to provoke my climax as fast and as often as possible. With her consent I shortened my walks through the woods in order to lengthen my rest periods.

On the first night I didn't notice her taking any precautions at all—in those days the Pill didn't exist—and, fearing her inexperience, I asked her about it. The voice that came from the shadows was ironic as she answered that she knew what she was doing and that her competence was certainly greater than mine in this area. As a matter of fact, we talked very little, in or out of the blackness of the wide matrimonial bed. I don't remember hearing her pronounce my name, which I appreciated, since I always found it ridiculous. Nor did we allude to the professor again, but in the drowsiness of the rest periods his image haunted my thoughts. I spent the small amount of energy I had left reflecting on him, Helena, myself, us. Our explosive passion justified everything: we must face the husband with loyalty.

Four days had passed. The cries of birds brought to the permanent night of the bedroom a sign of approaching dawn in the real world. The moment had arrived to tell Helena that we must make a decision. Her voice had never been so tranquilly docile as when she answered me. The decision had already been made. I would leave this very morning, because the professor would be back in the afternoon. She did not love me. It had been nothing more than a caprice she wished to experience; well, she had experienced it. She did not regret it but she considered it finished. She had never betrayed her husband before and did not expect to do so again. If she changed her mind, she would let me know. I was forbidden to attempt any contact with her or the professor. She would tell him that I had been disrespectful and that she had been obliged to send me away, thus justifying my definitive separation from them. I mustn't bother myself with moral questions; the option was clear: I must either lose the professor's good opinion of me, or destroy my friend. If I got up immediately, I would have time to shave, pack my bag, drink a glass of milk with some crackers, and catch the seven o'clock bus. The ticket with my seat number was in the drawer of the dresser in my room. The milk was in the refrigerator and the crackers in the cupboard, inside the tin with a parrot painted on it. She would not see me off. The good-byes had been said and she would stay in the bedroom until I was gone. Never had Helena talked so much. I followed all her instructions to the letter, including the crackers and milk. I left in such a daze that it was only upon arriving in São Paulo that I remembered it was my twenty-fifth birthday.

During the seconds that it took me to approach the old professor as he rose from the stone bench in the dwarf-decorated park, I relived thirty years' worth of feelings. At first, my love for Helena and my shame toward the professor had all been one, making me a miserable creature no longer interested in Hitler's victories, my work, women, or life itself. In the second phase, I thought sometimes of Helena, sometimes of the professor. When it was Helena's turn, the absurd hope of her seeking me once more—a possibility she herself had raised that morning when she had said good-bye—would inundate me. Thoughts of Professor Alberto, on the other hand, made my imagination take flight. I am convinced that it was because of him that I began to hate fascism. I tried to enlist in the army; I dreamed of dying a nationally recognized hero with my picture in all the papers so he would find out and would pardon me. As time passed, my ardor for Helena began to cool under the power of substitutes. But during those thirty years there was no shame, personal or national, that could rival that brought about by the image of the professor. At the very instant I bent over to shake his hand, shame invaded the deep wrinkles of my face with a red flush, juvenile and intact, as bright as the scarlet-tinted beret worn by the dwarf among the rosebushes. Upon closer inspection, I could evaluate the devastation of the old teacher's face; it was much greater than one would suppose for the seventy-odd years I ascribed him. If I recognized him in the park from a distance of several yards it was due to the growing twilight, which transmitted only his silhouette, familiar to me exactly because I hadn't seen him for thirty years and had thought about him daily. Meeting him suddenly in full light, I would have recognized him only with difficulty. As he spoke my name, he made a gesture as if to introduce Helena, whom I only then recognized. Unlike the professor, she had become harder to recognize from a distance; she was a shadow with its limbs folded up, intimidated by rheumatism. Her face, seen close up, was still smooth and much like its original, which time had blurred in my memory. Our hands barely touched, mutual reluctance augmented by arthritic precaution. She never stopped staring tranquilly at me the entire time, her eyes charged with investigation. As for the professor, his effusive expressions of the old fondness were marked by unconcealable signs of discomfort. I have forgotten what we said in the course of this brief encounter, except for a few surprising political allusions. At one point he affirmed that if he were the right age, he would be robbing banks and assaulting headquarters like . . .

His hesitation was provoked by Helena, who placed an arthritic hand on his shoulder. I looked more attentively at the old man's face, trying to figure out the meaning of this game, and to my alarm discovered delirium emanating from his eyes and causing his lips to twitch. The crisis was over quickly, but it drained the professor, who, after a moment of panting to catch his breath, proposed to Helena that they retire. I went with them along the street and across the small bridge, which had been named for a forgotten poet. We stopped before a hotel with an indigenous name: Jerubiçaba. The old man pointed to a tablet, where I read that "jerubiçaba" in the language of the Tupi Indians meant "loyalty." I once again felt the blood rush to tint my wrinkles, but he only commented, with the apparent fastidiousness of erudition, that the Tupi of the hotel corporation didn't inspire his confidence any more than the Latin of the local clergyman. He added that he was an assiduous frequenter of the chapel there in Águas, where an aged priest persisted in saying the mass the old-fashioned way. The reference to loyalty was not, evidently, directed against me, and this idea relieved me, but the relief didn't last. Frightened, I perceived that the professor was making ironic remarks to gain time: he intended to tell me something of grave importance, he announced. I waited, chilled. He reflected a little, looking at the ground, and began to speak in a voice so soft that to hear him I almost had to put my face against his. Removed a little from her husband's whispers, Helena took advantage of the opportunity and bade me farewell with a discreet movement of her head. The terrible hour of judgment, awaited for thirty years, had arrived. Helena's departure, however, left the professor almost helpless. He leaned on my arm with such force that for an instant I had the impression that he was going to attack me. Then quickly he calmed himself and his voice became clearer. As for me, this postponement of the execution gave me time to gather courage for the attitude I meant to take. I would hear everything without saying a word; at the end I would kneel before him and, if he didn't push me away, I would kiss his hand.

He began by saying in a calm voice that the time and place weren't right for the long conversation he intended to have with me, but that we could meet on the following day. Electrified with hope—his tone made clear the certainty of pardon—I managed to stutter some word of recognition for the grace placed within my grasp. Yet as he continued, his words again silenced me, not so much from penitence as from alarm at the completely unexpected direction he took. Speaking with an increasing clarity that seemed impregnated with despair, he said that he had committed a crime and had paid dearly for it. The punish ment had been such that he could not conceive of anything worse. Even so, he hadn't found peace. He had gone back to the church of his childhood, was trying to confess and receive communion daily, but his nature made him rebel daily as well, wanting to escape his incommensurably cruel chastisement, in spite of its being deserved. He passed his days in weighing the crime and the punishment on the balances of an insane scale. The fortuitous encounter with me seemed predestined, he added in great exultation. The remark about the ''insane scale'' put me on my guard: suddenly it occurred to me that the professor might be mentally deranged and I prepared myself to hear him out patiently. This new possibility would explain his confident cordiality ever since our meeting in the park; moreover, it revived in me pricks of remorse which now became irresolvable, since the pardon of a lunatic would be meaningless. His next words demonstrated to me that he had guessed my suspicions. He said that he could understand my uneasiness, that the confused generalities in which he was speaking must make him appear to be the victim of some morbid delirium. But unfortunately this wasn't the case; he wasn't demented, the facts existed and they were unchangeable. On the following day I would find out about everything and could judge for myself. We agreed to meet in the little park at sunset. Excessively bright light was bad for him.

. As I went slowly up the landscaped ramp leading to the Grand Hotel, my mind was racked with agitation, which had lasted through the night and was finally overcome only by fatigue in the wee hours of the morning. When I awoke, I was immediately assaulted by the anxiety of the evening before, and my tension increased as the hour of the meeting approached. Seated on the same bench as on the previous evening was Helena, alone. She was looking with interest at the remains of a plaster dwarf, only two small yellow boots contrasting with the green of the lawn. It had been toppled either by the wind or by some tourist insensible to the simple prettiness of the spa. She began by saying that the professor was not feeling well and had spent the day in bed; but that this wasn't the only reason he had failed to come. In truth, after meeting me again he couldn't find the strength to converse with me further. He had asked Helena to do it for him, to tell me everything, everything, and she was ready to carry out her mission to the letter. There were, however, a large number of details surrounding an important fact that she didn't know and refused to probe into. She insisted, moreover, that I let her speak without interruption, not only to make her task easier but also because she would exhaust the subject at hand to such an extent that no query could possibly remain unanswered.

All my earlier sentiments had now been replaced by such curiosity that for the moment the identity of Helena herself was forgotten. I believe the same thing happened with her: as soon as she began to speak, my personality dissipated, though her eyes never once left my face. She spoke slowly in an almost continuous stream, taking care to forget nothing, so methodical that she never needed to go back to fill in something she had already covered. Helena's somewhat declamatory manner of expressing herself held a literary familiarity for me, and as I tried to recall the name of the writer whom she resembled, I discovered that it was myself, the unpublished author of numerous writings in an old-fashioned, at times pompous, style. Her manner remained severe during the entire course of her narrative, and the ironies that occasionally sprang up were intrinsic to the facts she was relating, never calculated to provoke the affliction I again now felt.

''Alberto loved only three persons in his life. The first was you, and if you hadn't gone abroad and I hadn't come along, you would probably have been the only one. This was even more extraordinary because I doubt that anyone exists who has more love to give than he. I cannot explain why, but I know that his feelings for his parents and brothers never went beyond the requirements of convention. His so-called friends, from childhood, youth, and adulthood, were numerous but inconstant, and were merely companions for play, study, or conversation. This psychological block was undoubtedly profound but not insurmountable, since with only your reserve and directness you managed to strike home to his immense reserves of stored-up affection. From first making your acquaintance when you were in grammar school until you left for Europe, you were the center of his life. He never held anything back from you, he even found your name attractive. When we met, it was I who fell in love first; he had thoughts only for his absent friend. How he lamented not having a picture of you! I love my husband today as much as ever and I am jealous by nature. And so, during more than thirty years of loving him, you were the only person of whom I was ever jealous. I liked Alberto the day I met him and I began to seek him out under the most varied pretexts. I think that he was happy to have me for company because he found me an attentive listener interested in stories about you. He read your letters out loud and made long comments, omitting from the narrative, as I later found out, one or two more scandalous adventures. He would talk laughingly about your innumerable sweethearts, about your insistence on introducing them to him one by one in order to get his opinion. My jealousy was probably unbecoming, but it was thanks to you that he came to know me better and to like me. In my urge to separate him from you I precipitated things; we became lovers one morning and that very afternoon he started getting our marriage papers in order. The motive for his haste to marry was the desire that I get pregnant as soon as possible, which I at first found touching, but then I grew cool when he said he wanted our child to be a boy just like you. From that moment our lives began to darken. Months passed and I didn't get pregnant. In his pride he blamed me. Only after having me examined by countless specialists who unanimously confirmed my capacity to reproduce did he resign himself to submit to similar examinations. He went to a dozen doctors and as many laboratories. Finally, accepting the fact that he was sterile, he grew closer to me than ever before. In all our thirty years together, it was in this period that we were most united; our thoughts and our reactions were like those of one person. Only this incredible identification with each other could have made possible the madness to which we resorted. The first time Alberto expounded the plan to me, I reacted with horror and ran crying to my confessor. I was and still am a Catholic; my religious beliefs have always been real in spite of their simplicity, remaining so in the face of my husband's atheism and even when I grew intellectually and became capable of knowledge, reflection, and self-expression. My confessor had previously become angry with me on two occasions, the first when I gave myself to Alberto before our marriage, the second for not persuading my husband to marry in the Church. This time, he lost his temper and shouted at me. According to him I was being induced by the devil to challenge God's will directly and to commit a crime against my neighbor. And if I became an accomplice in my husband's perverse scheme, he said, there would be no more place for me in the Catholic church; *he* at any rate forbade me to mention it to him again—within the confessional or without. But he didn't follow through with this prohibition, continuing—with sorrow—to receive, hear, and counsel me in the confessional, sacristy, and parish house, even as late as last year when he died of old age. I discussed my confessor's arguments with Alberto. With his usual clarity, he established a difference between the priest's two statements. He made sarcastic remarks about believing in the possibility of human defiance of God, an idea which could only spring from the diabolic sin of pride, a subject on which he rightly considered himself an authority. He didn't jest, however, at the reference to the crime against one's neighbor. That was the point he came back to again and again during the weeks he spent persuading me. He easily destroyed my poor arguments, since he was, in fact, the patient and competent agency behind my line of reasoning. Today I can see clearly the method he used. First, he isolated God, showing him to be equally inaccessible to a believer or an atheist. Then he concentrated on the crime against his neighbor, that neighbor, of course, being you. For the sake of argument, he named himself the criminal and you the victim, and asked who would be more seriously hurt. He deliberately began the debate on the vulgar level of immediate appearances—he the cuckold and you the seducer. Next, he contrasted his own painful frustration with the impetuous enjoyment of sex you had described to him so often in letters and conversations. His reflections progressed to higher and higher levels until they reached a sphere of sublime spiritual values, which even today I recall as moving. The gravest consequence for both of you would be the mutual loss of friendship. Alberto analyzed how little this would mean to you, whose life was replete with the love of family, friends, and women; you who called forth affection by the simple act of living; you who had revealed an incredible capacity for new beginnings. Then he would approach the matter from the opposite angle, outlining all you meant to him. The comparison was irresistible. You would be merely a bit inconvenienced by a broken friendship, whereas he would be making a true sacrifice. He explained to me the need for this sacrifice in terms of a newly adopted, sincerely believed system of metaphysics that denied the scientific naturalism he had always embraced: he was one of those men destined to have little in any area of life. A mysterious law denied such individuals as himself the right to accumulation or variety; these could only be achieved through substitution. The figure two was his quota of love in this world and had been filled by myself and you. The love for a child would demand the sacrifice of one of us, you or me. Indeed, he told me something for which I've only recently forgiven him: that if he had gotten me pregnant, he would have found it harmonious for me to die in childbirth and the quota to be filled by you and the child. This perverse temper was rare. The sentiment of our unity generally prevailed, and based on that, Alberto discarded the counterproposal I made of our adopting a child. It seemed essential to him that the child should emanate from at least one half of the single being we constituted. I don't need to say more, because the person exterior to us, indispensible even if temporary, could be no one other than yourself. I must admit that the dark side of my personality played a role in what happened: tangled with fears and scruples of all kinds, there was one element in this madness that always excited me—you would disappear forever from Alberto's life.''

Without taking her eyes from me, Helena stopped

talking for an instant. I didn't say anything and she proceeded.

"I don't believe it's necessary to explain in minute detail the project he had planned, since you are as familiar with its execution as I am. What made everything easier was the extraordinary knowledge he had of you. He had observed that the girls who most attracted you—in life, in illustrated magazines, or on the movie screen—all had one thing in common: when they laughed one could see the beginning of their upper gums. I was never the type who laughed much and when I did, I hardly opened my mouth. I had to submit myself to painful exercises in front of the mirror until I could force my aching muscles to wrinkle up my lip in the necessary position. The cinema, which he has always detested, was also useful. You would drag him to see films—only you could— and Alberto amused himself with your enthusiasm for hairdos that elongated the neck and dresses that unabashedly insinuated the curves of the body. Not since your departure for Europe had he set foot in a theater, but he began going again with me, guided by the photos on display, making me pay close attention to the actresses' gowns and way of walking. He completed the indoctrination with numerous copies of sensational magazines, most of them printed in English. We went to shops looking for yard goods; I myself took on the job of cutting and sewing because I couldn't bear the absurdity of ordering such a dress from a seamstress. I'm good at sewing but I had to remake that outlandish getup five times. The rehearsals were even longer, first in São Paulo and later in the setting of the cottage in Campos do Jordão. The dress rehearsal, extremely tiring, ended only an hour before you arrived. On that occasion, the diversity of Alberto's talents was once again manifested. I think he might have made a great director, and in the episode I'm recalling, the only obstacle that his creativity could not surmount was my incompetence as an actress. You undoubtedly found me an incoherent, restless, and capricious woman, when the character called for should have been above all welcoming and warm. Even so, what little I managed to do I owe to the pertinacity and—why not say it?—genius of my husband. The moment I came 'on stage,' when you rang the doorbell, I was overcome by such a fit of nerves that I almost gave up the whole thing. I marshaled all my strength, but I felt like an automaton about to fall to pieces. The failure of the opening scene altered the script and I was obliged to improvise. I'm aware that I came across badly, but at least I conquered the obstacle that almost caused the plan to fail: your unexpected decision to wait for Alberto's return at the home of your relatives in Capivari. I managed to control myself, but in order to carry out my job during four miserable, interminable days and nights I had to modify completely the character that had been composed with such care and imagination. I used very little of the long text he had written and which I knew by heart, having been obliged to recite it over and over again at the table, in bed, and during my leisure hours. You helped me a great deal at the first dinner when you talked the whole time, telling stories that I didn't hear, worried as I was with wrinkling my upper lip to show my gums when I laughed. In bed, silence was easier for me and I could dispense with the heavily erotic lines that Alberto had translated and adapted from special French books. The rest of the time, thank goodness, you agreed uncomplainingly to go for walks through the surrounding countryside or rest in the guest room. I can truly say that prior to the tragedy which befell us, that period with you was the worst of my whole life. It would have been totally unbearable if it hadn't been for your manner of submissively accepting the rules of the game without the slightest displeasure, even though I imposed them more authoritatively than I ever imagined I could. I feel that I'm probably attributing more merit than is due to myself and you, whereas it is only to Alberto that we owed the perfect development of the unhappy business. My poor and noble husband deserved that everything go well. The amount of attention he gave to ridiculously minute details will give you an idea of the determination, work, and expense he put into this. He knew what you most enjoyed eating and was greatly upset at not finding partridges and guinea hens available for that evening. He was saved by your letters from Europe, which he always consulted and in which you raved about *canard aux oranges*. The wines had been stored up for you long before the fatal night, but the champagne you wrote about on a picture postcard of the Reims cathedral was acquired with painful effort and considerable money. He was convinced that this champagne and no other must play a decisive part in that first dinner, the crucial chapter in the plot. In São Paulo, no wine dealer had heard of that brand; Alberto traveled to Rio in search of it, which was reasonable, but he extended his search all the way to Porto Alegre, having been led astray by mistaken information. He consulted wine connoisseurs to no avail and finally, disposed to go to any lengths, he tried the society editors. One of them informed him that a few dozen bottles of the famous brand were the glory of the wine cellar at the Jockey Club of Argentina. Alberto considered making the trip to Buenos Aires, but then he remembered that one of the wine experts he had consulted, a professor of literary theory, was planning to go there. This professor received him and the favor he asked with mild surprise, since he hardly knew Alberto. But as the man was amiable and sympathetic to anything concerning wines, he took it upon himself to carry out the difficult mission, which involved the bribery of an English maître d'hôtel, a venerable figure among the Buenos Aires upper crust. Yet in spite of this laborious acquisition of the champagne, it isn't the final example of his meticulousness, because it was mainly a shock tactic. Much subtler was the choice of the dessert. The duck and the wines were a direct appeal to your appetite and good taste, and effectively laid the groundwork for the maternal comforts of a homey pudding served in a wide dish. The function of the dessert was largely psychological; it was to provoke the subconscious mechanism of your memory, so vibrant as it was to sensual connotations. At first, Alberto had chosen figs, but back then they weren't as high quality as the ones they cultivate these days in Valinhos. This difficulty in finding decent figs was fortuitous because it led to an incomparably more refined solution. He was well aware of an affair you had had just before your trip to Europe, that woman with the bubbling laugh and the exposed gum who, according to your confidences, had had more powerful sex appeal for you than any other. You couldn't forget her, and your disappointment at finding out she had married was enormous. Several times Alberto had gone to restaurants with the two of you, and observed that she liked to vary the menu but that for dessert she always ordered caramel pudding. I think he was right to insist—in the face of my skepticism—that this dessert, humble in the eyes of most, must have acquired for you an emotional charge of the most explosive sort. When I gave him the complete report on the four days spent in the cottage, I conceded that the caramel pudding had been a more conclusive factor than the dress, the wine, or my gum to attract you to the kitchen when it was time for after-dinner coffee—in an acutely indiscreet state that would normally have constrained any well-bred person. But then, it would be inaccurate to say that Alberto and my preparations were inspired exclusively by the direct observation of life. We read and studied a great deal, especially Alberto, who single-handedly took on the foreign-language texts, an area in which I was never very strong except for Spanish and French. The erotic books taught us that a meal accompanied by fine wines is stimulating, but that repetition of such a repast is counterproductive. A large part of this reading was useless, since most of the material was devoted only to imparting the prolongation of stimuli to the limit of tolerance, refinements which had no practical use for our ends. As for us, we were always frugal with sex. Since our objective regarding you was simple, the innocent observation of nature sufficed, and it was in this area that I made my modest contribution. I am the granddaughter and daughter of farming people, and I spent my childhood in the midst of horses and cattle. I was amazed to read, in the Spanish translation of a Scandinavian book, the illustrated description of a method very much like the manipulations to which stallions are submitted to increase their breeding capacity while shortening the time required for their function.''

This time Helena paused slightly longer. Her voice

had become hoarse. She moved closer to be able to speak more softly. Her eyes had changed; they were not merely directed toward me, but were scrutinizing me closely, completely attentive to my presence.

''Alberto was terribly worried about your health. Certain passages from a letter in which you scoffed at the French doctors gave rise to his suspicion that you had contracted some venereal disease in Paris. But it wasn't only that which led him to subject you to so many examinations. From our own experience with doctors, we had learned that the proportion of sterile men is much higher than is commonly supposed. It was absolutely necessary that we be certain of your reproductive capacity, without which all our patient effort would have been useless and, worse, ridiculous. Once your virility was established, the days planned for our time together were chosen with precision. The only thing Alberto couldn't manage to remember was the rhythm of my menstrual flux. He underlined my dates on a small calendar that he consulted, slightly embarrassed, when he fixed the date on which we would meet in Campos do Jordão. He relaxed only when you reminded him that you would be celebrating your birthday with us. In spite of all our planning, we feared the intervention of some unforeseeable factor, and for this reason it was decided that when you and I parted, the possibility of further encounters would not be discouraged. We considered the possibility of having me look you up again—several times if necessary. It wasn't. Our son was born at normal term, exactly nine months, day for day, hour for hour, from the time you left the cottage. I am sure that if you had left one day earlier, the whole thing would have had to be done over. Starting from the instant that my pregnancy was confirmed, we never again mentioned your name. What's more, I know that during fifteen years he never even thought about you, which led me to believe in this strange theory of his quota of loved ones being limited to two. Yet the devotion and love with which he inundated my son's life and mine had such volume and force that it alone would have accelerated the transformation of the world, given the unthinkable hypothesis of one's being able to participate therein. As for myself, before we met I knew you exclusively through Alberto, a knowledge that had never had a visual reference. We had no pictures of you in our home, and to go forward with the task I had undertaken, it was essential that I not look at you. For the first few minutes, I had to watch myself, but afterward not seeing you became automatic. In bed, the darkness facilitated things, but I had other motives for choosing the dark. To kiss you without seeing you would be easier than an hour and a half spent avoiding your face over dinner, although I managed to do that on the first evening. If there were a technical necessity—say, if you had fallen into the category of the obsessive visual erotics classified by Kerner (an improbability according to my husband)—I would have turned on the lights in order to expose my nudity as long and as often as necessary. My sense of shame would not have been offended, since it had gone off with Alberto and only returned after you left. If I arranged the darkness, it was because I didn't feel I had the right to hide the small statues of Our Lord and the saints that always accompany me. At the same time, I couldn't tolerate their seeing or being seen by the stranger at my side. They had no part in all that; I always kept God rigorously out of the scheme, even to the point that during

those days, I never once stopped saying my prayers.
But I never asked for divine help to get pregnant. In
short, because I didn't see you, you remained unknown to me in form, even in flesh, since I was always too busy concentrating on my work to feel your
weight or penetration. You were an easily forgotten
abstraction. I probably felt an unconscious need to
blot you out completely. Later, when memory
brought things back one by one, Alberto and I decided that if your death had indeed occurred, con-
firming your total disappearance, there might have
been hope for us. He abandoned this idea at once, but
I did not. In my mature years, I stopped agreeing un-
conditionally with all my husband's views, though I
never failed to recognize his overwhelming superiority. We leaned in different directions according to the
shadings of our temperaments, my husband's proud
and self-castigating, mine much quieter. In our happy
years, the result of this difference was to fuse us together in the joy of being parents. I would not know
how to describe the happiness the child brought us.
And it would be cruel to speak of it. From babyhood
our child was an exact replica of all Alberto's good
qualities, added to which he had a wonderful disposi-
tion, toward everyone and everything with which my
poor husband never got acquainted. As an adolescent, he was talent and virtue incarnate—a beautiful
young man. The darkening of Alberto's nature dates
from this time. His face took on a look of diffuse apprehension and soon acquired the contours of prema-
ture old age. Since it was always he who took
command of our conversations, I waited quietly, always fearing that he would actually reveal what was
on his mind. His changed humor began to create
crises, always heralded by his behavior at the table;

he would stare fixedly at the boy to the point of embarrassing him. Afterward, Alberto would get up in silence and spend hours in the library writing numbers or—what was worse—locking himself in the bedroom to cry. Our son possessed the somewhat ambiguous gracefulness that comes with puberty and, remembering our old readings about sex, I asked myself if what was bothering Alberto could be the fear that the boy was a homosexual. But the boy, whom I still regarded as a child, soon found a girl friend and began a relationship in keeping with the pattern of today's young people. Still Alberto remained tense and silent. As time went on, the boy spent less and less time at home. The university, the girl, his job, his numerous friends, a great many commitments that I knew nothing about, and finally the apartment that he rented with his girl friend, all prevented our seeing him often. He would have dinner with us on the occasions of his and our birthdays. I didn't complain, understanding how painful it must be for a young man like him to witness his father's inexplicable suffering. It was with the grestest dismay that I would examine the wastebasket, full of wadded-up pages: numbers, nothing but numbers arranged in the most varied compositions and accompanied by the plus or minus sign; devoid, however, of any arithmetic function. The calculations were of a sort that was beyond me. He read imported books with an obsession; they too were inaccessible to me due to their language and style. Although my preoccupation grew I never thought of forcing him to see a doctor, because I knew my husband was not mad. But he gave that impression, principally at our son's birthday parties and to such an extent that I thought about canceling these dinners. It was not necessary. On the day that he was twenty-five years old, the boy and his fiancée did not appear at the dinner that I had prepared with special attention and sadness, resolved as I was that it would be the last one. The approach of this birthday had brought on a stronger than usual crisis in Alberto: he withdrew into total silence, not even touching the meals that I took to him in bed. His going down to dinner was out of the question, which relieved me considerably. On this unfortunate night I went up to our bedroom to get ready, wanting to present an agreeable appearance to the young people. I was happy to hear Alberto's voice, although he spoke in a tone of panic. He said that *if* our son should arrive, he wanted to be told, but he didn't wish to see him that night; he should come back the next day. I wondered what this "if" might mean, and thought about it again when, much later, I was dining alone at the nearly untouched flower-adorned table. At a certain moment I perceived that Alberto had gotten up and was listening, panting, to the silence of the house. A few minutes later, I heard strange sounds and I ran to the bedroom where I found him with his eyes popping out of his head, in a state that appeared to be one of agony. During the following weeks I thought only of Alberto's survival and I did only one thing—fight for his life. The doctors could not diagnose his illness, and did nothing more than skeptically write prescriptions for trivial medicines. If he didn't die, it was because I didn't let him, and also because he didn't want to leave me. As soon as he grew better, I went to my son's apartment in Vila Buarque but the doorkeeper only knew that the young couple had moved some time before. I tried to find out more from the man, telling him who I was, that the father of the young man was very ill, and that I needed to inform him. Could he tell me of some neighbor or friend? I had to find out his new address. The man, who came from the Northeast, merely shrugged his shoulders; he could tell me nothing more. I returned home beside myself, but Alberto, who was emerging little by little from his fatigue and silence, asked me nothing. Now his convalescence was unexpectedly quick. He gained new energy and soon began to go out daily, on trips the purpose of which I never knew. He also started to worry a lot about me again, trying to calm me with respect to our son's disappearance. Then one day he told me that the boy had been arrested but added that I should not worry excessively, the arrest of young people had become commonplace. Yes, he had already taken certain actions; one must stay calm. Finally, with infinite caution, he told me that our son had died—on his birthday. It was Alberto's turn to take care of me and not allow me to die. His battle was far harder, because I had no scruples about dying and leaving him alone. When I had once again been restored to the world (though I was victimized by attacks of arthritis so painful that they actually diverted my thoughts) Alberto resumed his travels, sometimes spending months away from home. I'm certain he found out about everything, absolutely everything and, in keeping with his character, was only satisfied when he exhausted all the possible sources of information. I learned only that my son had been arrested under a false name—which I was never told—and that a few days later he died in prison. I never allowed myself to know more, and even during his most violent ravings, Alberto always respected my ignorance. On the two or three occasions such as last night when, already skirting delirium, he came close to forgetting himself, the touch of my hand was enough to make him stop. As I have never allowed myself any exercise of the imagination, I shall go to my grave knowing only that my son was arrested and that he died on the day he turned twenty-five. I made an exception in the case of his fiancée and asked questions. I learned that she also had been arrested and had lost her mind. One of her grandfathers is rich and she is now hospitalized in Switzerland, probably for the rest of her life, which I pray to God will be short. Alberto completed his mission and returned home; since then he has left only twice a year to accompany me here. Lately he has been attending the earliest mass of the day in the Perdizes parish. He has never again opened a book; he reads only inside himself, collecting material for his ceaseless reflections—he has never been so talkative. Before the tragedy he already considered himself to blame for everything, and he has not wavered from this fundamental belief. He arrived at it by elaborating in succession various theses which, removing the variations and combinations, can be reduced to two; one, already imagined before our son's death, and the other, which he definitively embraced. They boil down to the same thing: he committed a crime and his punishment was the death of the boy. What distinguishes one thesis from the other is the nature of the crime. The starting point was the old idea of the quota of people he had a right to love in this world, with the cipher two implacably present. He had gotten this notion from numerology, a science which, as usual, he later studied exhaustively. This worry, which as you know had such importance for us at the time we decided to provide ourselves with a child, disappeared during our son's first years and youth. Today I ask myself if what unleashed Alberto's imagination wasn't an eventual resemblance he saw between our son and you. I have no way of knowing if the man I went to bed with in Campos do Jordão but never saw was like my son. These last two days I've been scrutinizing you, trying to figure out if my son, when he grew older, would have resembled you. But this is an absurd effort because he'll always be twenty-five years old until the moment of his second and final death, when Alberto and I leave this world. The part played by the figure twenty-five in the drama was decisive. In numerology, the combination between the two and the five can be fatal, and when Alberto remembered that you turned twenty-five on the exact day you made me pregnant, he never again stopped his research and calculations in the hope of seeing the invariably ill-fated omens annulled by some error. The coincidence of dates and ages, too incredible to be mere coincidence, strengthened Alberto's theory in my view. From then on, it wasn't hard to convince me that the crime denounced by my husband's numerological science had been committed above all against you. Alberto did not have the right to displace you, nor me for that matter, in his affection. We were irremovable and his love for us untransferable. Any disobedience whatsoever would directly violate the Great Law, which had marked and warned him with the one incontrovertible sign: sterility. Believing that he had the right to substitute another person as long as he respected the prescribed quota, Alberto cheated, with the added offense of designating to the person unfairly eliminated—you— the job of sowing the seed for the substitution itself. He trespassed even deeper into the forbidden zone. Through some sign I was unaware of, he became alarmed at the crime he had committed and thought about putting you back into the position you formerly occupied. But it was too late. The substitute—our son—was about to be born and, lost in the hellish maze, my poor and intrepid husband wished that through my death the quota to which he had the right would be filled by our son and you. Later, delirious with the hope that somehow the alchemy of life might be duped, he ardently hoped that you had died, so that the trinity composed of himself, our son, and me might not be altered. This notion led Alberto to abandon the first thesis that I not only accepted, but to which I remain faithful in spite of his persuasive dialectic and the chidings of my confessor. It was the first time my husband did not manage to break down my train of reasoning. This failure confirms his merit and ability as a teacher, for it seems to me almost miraculous that I should have been able to confront him, my own mediocrity being what it is. With the priest I had less trouble maintaining my position, since once I discovered I could not make him understand the duplicity of the universe, I kept his sphere of knowledge separate from my husband's. At any rate, it was the idea of trinity that led Alberto to adopt the position that he today defends. He sought to probe the nature of the contradiction between the three and the two. The possibility of a fusion between the three and the one seemed transparent to him. On the rare occasions that he attempted to find analogous terms for the Unrevealed Truth, he concluded with his usual optimism that there should be no reasons for its contradicting the Revealed Truth. If the three and the one attract each other irresistibly, the reciprocal revulsion between the two and the three is also uncontrollable. When he completed the deeper theoretical study of the problem, he believed he had found the key to the understanding of his destiny. He had erroneously interpreted the number two as his quota by ascribing to himself the faculty of loving and being loved by up to two people. In reality, he had the right to only one, since his pride—or more precisely his self-love—had already filled half of his quota from the start. It is not up to me to argue with him about this last idea, which offers no loophole. If I resist him it is because I am moved to tears by the overwhelming and fragile humanity Alberto emits, his heroically humane willingness not only to assume all the blame of the world but also, always, to restrict his own rights to life, defense, and protest. The conviction to which he has come has the merit, aside from all the others, of promoting the gradual pacification of his spirit. You and our son having been sacrificed, leaving only him and me, he now knows that I did not constitute still one more ponderous threat to the universal equilibrium. His rebelliousness has almost dissipated, and yesterday's episode was an exception that will not be repeated. It was caused by the impact of meeting you, a happening filled with potential consequences that we must not risk. If the reciprocal love between Alberto and you should be reborn, everything will start over again. Yesterday's meeting was the last one. My twenty-five days' cure has only begun, and Águas de São Pedro is too small for the three of us. I insist that you leave today. I want to make it clear that Alberto and I do not expect you to condemn or to absolve us, for you will understand that you have neither the authority nor the ability to judge. In order to protect us from any possible trick of fate that might take advantage of Alberto's fragile humanity, I shall say that you did not respect the gravity of the situation, that you mocked us for being two dithering lunatics. I must now hurry back to him; in these last few years I have never left him alone for so long a time. I realize that there are only two people in the world who deserve this sacrifice: the insane fiancée and yourself. Farewell.''

Stunned by astonishment and emotion, I did not notice that Helena had left me. When I found myself alone on the bench, surrounded by dwarfs, I ran at once toward my hotel, crossing through the center of the lawn to gain time. The hillside there is steeper than near the driveway; I arrived at the front desk too breathless to talk and had to catch my breath before announcing that I was leaving and wanted my bill. The receptionist looked at me with surprise, without understanding what I was trying to say. I realized that in the last few hours I had misplaced the habit of speech, and I needed to concentrate for the words to resume their customary function.

As I drove back to São Paulo, the roads clear at that hour of the night, the amount of attention needed to drive the car did not interfere with the course of my thoughts. I at once abandoned the picture in my head of Helena's pathetic face and the tragic figure of the professor to fix instead upon the son that I had gained and lost in so short a time. The skeletal outline of his existence—birth, studies, love, battle, death, and martyrdom—threw an immense emptiness over me that only his memory could fill. This idea made me go back to the other interpreters of our drama. When I say ''our'' I am conscious of my pretentiousness, since I was hardly more than an extra. But I decided to prolong my part, since I could not commit the memory of my son to the custody of three insane people: one locked up in Switzerland, the other two calmly

completing the cycle of their madness here in São
Paulo. I decided to ask my son to save and enrich
me, and thus I am prepared to do anything, even to
seeing Helena and the professor again. As this isn't
possible, I need to take maximum advantage of the
weeks they will be staying in Águas de São Pedro.

Upon arriving home, I spent the rest of the night
thinking about the situation and writing this narrative, which will be my defense if I'm caught house-
breaking in Pacaembu. I am going there now, this
morning, the twenty-fifth day of the month, on
which I am completing my fiftieth year and com-
memorating for the first time the date of my son's
conception and death. Barring some unforeseen
event, I will not come back without at least a picture
of him and some books I need to study. This accumulation of birthdays, the day of the month which I
only now have noticed, and which multiplied by
two equals the number of years I've lived, all of this
tends to increase the agitation that has taken hold
of the very depths of my being but will not impede
my leaving for Pacaembu in two minutes, three at
the most. To get there from Alto dos Pinheiros
should take me twenty-five minutes. The possibility of recognizing and eventually being recognized
by Helena's holy images is a matter of indifference
to me.

To this document I sign my whole name instead
of just the initial ''P'' that I customarily put before
my surname. I am in fact called Polydoro, a favor-
able combination of five consonants and three
vowels (whose relationship the new orthography
alters), a clownish name given me in honor of an il-
lustrious great-grandfather, a name that doomed

my aspirations to harmony and elegance in a cruel and arbitrary world, the secret logic of which I have been ignorant of until today in spite of the rare opportunity afforded me: to know the great professor.

SECTION TWO

Ermengarda with an H

*E*RMENGARDA occupied my life for years and years on end and would occupy it still if it hadn't been for one of those things that interrupt the continuity of marriage and prohibit any going back. The verb *to occupy* was never used so perfectly as here. The dictionary sets forth its various meanings as: to take possession of, to be in possession of, to inhabit, to take, to fill, to be the object of, to attract, to practice, to have the right to, to invade, to extend oneself over, to employ, etc. Ermengarda installed herself comfortably in me from the time we were thirty until we were forty-odd years old. We were the same age.

She could never tolerate the idea that, although I was single, I couldn't marry her, which means that she always considered it my fault that she had had, before me, a legal husband. When I met her she was already separated from him, with a grown son whose legal guardianship had been entrusted to the father. The latter I never saw or learned anything about. She never referred to him; she didn't have time, since she talked only about herself. She wasn't exactly pretty, yet she had a beauty of the type in vogue during my mother's youth: a rosy complexion that inspired confidence. Only later did I come to evaluate the frenetic activity that flourished behind her old-fashioned composure.

Having notarized with flashy Paraguayan seals the expensive official papers in Spanish (with which Ermengarda refused to dispense) I took her, with the best of intentions, to my old house in Alto dos Pinheiros. A morally painful experience in my youth had made me an attentive and delicate man, a little timid, convinced that I owed others more than they owed me, or than I owed myself. My view of married life was simple, healthy, and serene. Work all day to increase one's assets; two children; instructive outings on Sundays and holidays; annual vacations at quiet beaches. Later, when the war was over, travel. An occasional adventure that might offer itself would be welcomed, without danger of its continuing. In short, my youthful dreams of supreme elegance, power, and culture had been reduced to a typical São Paulo level. Another element in this pleasant imaginary picture was the anticipation of evenings dedicated to military and political study, my amateur specialty. I could even do a little writing, another old fancy of mine of which traces still remained.

Very few men were disposed to be such good husbands as I; that was the source of the whole catastrophe. Ermengarda, among other wrong women, got put in the right place: by my side. My company caused her to blossom and bear with rare abundance. Never did a man owe so much annoyance to only one woman.

The first unpleasantness occurred on the day she moved in. I should explain in advance that I've always had a horror of my first name. I sign only the initial. I paid a fat bribe to the consul to omit it from the marriage certificate; and everywhere I go, people have the delicacy to call me by my surname. Ermengarda managed not to call me anything until the afternoon she came to live at Alto dos Pinheiros. She pronounced the house she knew so well too big, and the swimming pool she had never entered a luxury for social climbers. The main thing was that to say this, she addressed me repeatedly by my given name. Soon after we had met, when I slept with her for the first time, I had confessed this name to her as a retribution of the trust she had placed in my word, going to bed with me before assuring herself of a clearly defined state of affairs. The revelation of the secret was a symbol of my giving myself to her just as she had given herself to me. Thus the sacred ritual of marriage was exchanged for something more meaningful than the pompous certificate issued a few weeks afterward by some *gobierno civil* or other, probably kept in existence by a military regime. So I was shocked when, in the prelude of our union that had been officialized by a neighboring and friendly country, Ermengarda pronounced the four fatal syllables. And repeated them. When I started to protest, she got one jump ahead of me, saying that she liked me just as I was, without adding or subtracting so much as a comma—or a name, she added maliciously. Nevertheless she was a fanatic for truth, and it was true my name really was that. But that name and that truth, I argued, were our secret and belonged exclusively to our most intimate moments—it was an insult to modesty to voice it in front of the servants. Ermengarda did not prolong the discussion. She merely replied, smiling kindly, that she would accept living in the enormous house, she would accept the inconvenience of the swimming pool, which would only serve as an enticement for my brothers and other parasites who didn't have

41

anywhere else to go on Sundays, but that there were one or two points regarding my character that would definitely have to be changed. I needn't be frightened; she didn't intend to meddle in my life; everything would happen in such a gradual way that I wouldn't even notice. In fact I noticed clearly a few days later when she gave me a nickname—a nickname which wasn't really a nickname, but rather a shortened form of the hateful appellation. She merely amputated the last two syllables, and the effect this had on me was particularly agonizing, for the abbreviation sounded to me like a portent of the whole name. Later I continued to be sensitive only to the ridiculousness of the word *Poly*, a cat's name imposed on myself, who detested cats. But I accepted being called Poly not only by her but by her relatives, friends, and acquaintances who crowded the swimming pool on hot, bright Sundays. *Doro*, the rest of the name, turbid syllables full of black magic, remained hovering in the air, ready to stab me treacherously from Ermengarda's lips. This would invariably happen on one of the mornings when the pool was swarming with senior citizens, young people, and children, making it repugnant to dive into its promiscuous waters. However, the diabolical *doro* never attacked, because of the precaution I took of sticking close to Ermengarda's side, thus preventing her from yelling to me in her strident voice. The fact that she never went into the pool facilitated this maneuver and on many occasions I blessed a certain detail which I had not initially understood: Ermengarda did not care for water, using it even in day-to-day life with embarrassing frugality. In contact with her skin the finest French perfumes acquired a singular odor, recognizable among thousands. Having explained the origin of the name Poly, I must add that for years she referred to our discussion about it as an example of those mutual concessions without which the best marriages go to pieces. She would add that, naturally such concessions by themselves were not enough; they must be a reflection of a previous understanding. The only example she presented of our understanding was the aversion we both harbored for domestic animals. She cited it continually, even after having made an exception in the case of the cat proffered by the consul of Guatemala. I took a dislike to the creature at first sight, and for years I made an effort to ignore its presence; I didn't even know its name. One day the butler nervously asked me if I had happened to see Pafúncio, Pafúncio had run away. My joy was enormous when I realized what he was talking about. But the cat came back.

Abbreviating names was a habit she had. Since she talked so much she didn't have time to say peoples' full names, and she mutilated even those of her close relatives who came from Jundiaí and Campinas to spend weeks on end in the expensive new wing she insisted I build. Mother and Father were Mom and Pop, her paternal grandparents Grams and Gramps, her maternal grandmother Gran. Ermengarda's mother's father had died young, the victim of a fatal kick from a mule. Thus it was fortunately unnecessary for his future granddaughter to think up some ingenious nickname for him. She in turn disliked the dead and never mentioned them, much less addressed them. My business partner claims that this is a point on her side. I disagree with this opinion, but not because it favors Ermengarda. There were many things about her I admired, as will be seen. In the area of shortening names, for instance, her creativity was inexhaustible, especially when one bears in mind that the entire Christian and Tupi-Guarani nomenclatures were represented in the swimming pool, not to mention considerable sections of the Arabic, Judaic, and Oriental ones. Moreover, I admired the authority with which she imposed the abbreviations upon the person concerned and others within her immense circle of acquaintance. There was naturally an Isaura who became Isa and when a true Isa appeared she was easily accepted as Is. One day I was introduced at the gate of my house to the girl friend of one of her nephews, a girl who was also called Isa, who had been rechristened that very instant. I took off the hat that I actually wear and expressed my pleasure at meeting Miss I, repeating the name she herself spoke as she shook my hand. At that moment I was proud of Ermengarda.

The only inviolable name was her own. Progressive man that I am—that is, a supporter of all orthographic reforms—I had written Ermengarda without an *H* on the papers for our marriage outside Brazil. Her reaction was violent. She impugned the legal value (in fact, nonexistent) of the documents and demanded the reinstatement of the *H*. Everything had to be done over; I paid the fees again and if the papers didn't recross the Paraguayan border in the bellies of the diplomatic bags which carry the destiny of the Americas it was only because the functionaries at the consulate understood feminine caprice and were once again sensitive to the value of the cruzeiro as compared to their poor guarany. Ermengarda liked these people very much and the consul, his aides, and their fellow diplomats of Spanish or English tongue ended up as dedicated habitués of the swimming pool. Germans and Japanese came only before our break with the Axis powers or after the war ended. The Italians were out of the question; they didn't aspirate the *H* that Ermengarda demanded orally as well as in writing. She liked the company of refined people who accentuated the *H* naturally, and expected members of other linguistic sectors at least to pay her the deference of trying. Popular as she was among her subjects, it wasn't hard for them to scream her name incessantly, prolonging the *H* and the *R* as long as possible. On hot Sundays one could hear at distances of up to one hundred meters from the house the happy trill and croak of an unknown fauna.

For a while my throat resisted the effort demanded by the *H*, the beginning of an insubordination that was soon transformed into revolt and later into revolution and then all-out war. It was all very inward, in keeping with my nature. My capitulation in the skirmish over the *H* demonstrates the richness of her tactical resources. She had wanted us to share bedroom and bed, which flattered me in the beginning. Later I discovered that she couldn't go for long without hearing the sound of her own name. When the last visitors had left at night and the houseguests had retired to their apartments (incomparably superior to ours) it was my turn. Ermengarda always referred to herself in the third person, and thus never needed to abandon herself even when commenting on or asking about me or somebody else. I will never forget her voice during her attacks of insomnia, when she would wake me up to keep her company. "Do you think," she would say, "that Hermengarda doesn't realize your partner is robbing you? Hermengarda would not be Hermengarda if she hadn't caught on to the strategies of that so-and-so. Why doesn't he dare to set foot in our house anymore? Because he knows he's not fooling Hermengarda! Hermengarda is Hermengarda and when the others are going, Hermengarda is already on her way back. Why haven't your brothers come to swim in the pool? Because their wives—those little sisters-in-law you're so polite to—are envious of Hermengarda, of the dresses and jewels Hermengarda has, of Hermengarda's connections in the consulates. They're even envious of Hermengarda's husband! Hermengarda can see through things. Just wait and see if Hermengarda is right or not. What are your brothers always doing at the real estate agency, confabulating with your great friend, the thieving partner? And why do they get tongue-tied and embarrassed when Hermengarda appears? They think they can fool Hermengarda. Well, Hermengarda is not the fool in this house!''

When she finished, I was expected to speak. If her name didn't appear among my first words, she would shrink from me. There were nights when I wanted to be close to her. I still hoped to have children, and desire found a way around the obstacles that I have hinted at in this narrative. Nevertheless, Ermengarda would remain icy until I subjected myself to courting her out loud, supplicating: come on, let me, Hermengarda; please, Hermengarda, just a little; Hermengarda, only once, my Hermengarda! She would finally consent, but she insisted that I keep repeating her name with the *H*'s more and more aspirate. I would end up exhausted and hoarse.

I couldn't decide which was worse, the Sundays, dinners, and evening parties with the tribe, or the nights spent alone with my Mrs./mistress. Only at the real estate agency could I relax in the company of my partner, a faithful lifelong friend, or surrounded by the fraternal warmth of my brothers, who visited me in discreet and silent solidarity. There was also my secretary, an intelligent and understanding young woman. I got into the habit of taking her to lunch at the club while we went over current business. Her conversation was good for me; I even told her veiled confidences, naturally without mentioning Ermengarda's name. I was encouraged by the simple words she found to comment on the generalities I expressed. Perhaps the first impulses toward liberating action were thus formed, even though the crystallization of those impulses was only of a literary character.

Once in a while, after dinner, I would daringly leave the parents and grandparents to savor my cognac alone, behavior which Ermengarda could not tolerate, saying that I was being selfish. In our room, she would roar, ''Hermengarda has to haul all the weight. Hermengarda has to be well mannered for two. Hermengarda must be Hermengarda and Hermengarda's husband at one and the same time!'' Writing was still very important to me, and I would commit the audacity of abandoning the guests to satisfy my literary bent. I would sit in the library filling page after page for long delicious hours until the moment when Ermengarda would burst in complaining that Hermengarda was tired, Hermengarda wanted to go to bed, Hermengarda was going to bed, Hermengarda wanted me to go too, Hermengarda was a light sleeper, I should have more consideration for Hermengarda and remember that I would wake Hermengarda and Hermengarda wouldn't be able to get back to sleep. If I were less selfish I would think about

47

the next day, which was Saturday; I would remember what Saturdays and Sundays meant for Hermengarda, would think of Hermengarda's tribulations that would start at eight in the morning. Ermengarda would ask me, in short, to feel sorry for Hermengarda.

I was always sensitive to the charge of selfishness. My sense of guilt is sufficiently broad for me to comprehend that the fact of an accusation's being unjust doesn't mean that it is undeserved; it is only a matter of collecting by other means the secret debts one owes to the world. The loyalty that constitutes the best side of my character further weakened my position vis-à-vis Ermengarda. I couldn't deny her immense generosity: she was an excellent granddaughter, daughter, sister, aunt, cousin, niece, and friend. I'm sure she would have been an excellent mother if the child's father had given her an opportunity, which he didn't. Her being all this at my expense—and against my grain—placed me in a difficult position. To judge her I would be obliged to pit personal interest against the bloc of goodwill formed by the legion of her beneficiaries. If it weren't for my literary side I would never have freed myself from her. In general, I don't like what I write, but one night, inspired by the commemorations of the 1932 Revolution, I wrote a poem in honor of the women of São Paulo. I rather liked the poem, and I was anxious to talk with somebody about it, no matter who, when Ermengarda came in. Without thinking, I asked her to sit down and read aloud what I had written. For about thirty seconds she listened attentively to my "Eulogy to the São Paulo Lady," a title that interested her, since she had been born in Jundiaí. My São Paulo lady, however, was universal and timeless, now succoring the *bandeirante*

weary from hunting Indians, now encouraging the
volunteers of '32 when they straggled toward the rear
guard, alarmed by the shots. Unable to recognize herself in the text, as she wasn't given to hunting or revo-
lutions, Ermengarda at once began to show signs of
impatience. When she could contain herself no longer
she interrupted me brutally. She pronounced ''Poly''
with such vehemence that I feared she would come
out with my whole name. Decidedly, I only thought
about myself. Hermengarda, besides having to run
the absurdly large house single-handed, had to listen
to the nonsense that I scribbled instead of visiting
with the relatives whom we hadn't seen in almost a
month. And anyway, this business of eulogies to
ladies was completely out of style, nobody would be
interested in it except idiots like me. She poured out
this speech in a running stream and stomped up-
stairs.

To her surprise—and mine—I did not accompany
her. I remained in the library with my honor offended, not for the sake of São Paulo but for the sake
of my writing. I reread my poem carefully, then woke
up the butler and ordered him to prepare one of the
guest suites, the best in the new wing, exclusively reserved for the widowed grandmother. Our beloved
Gran was supposed to arrive the next day from Águas
de São Pedro, having gotten relief from her arthritis
thanks to the treatment that Ermengarda's generosity
had provided for her at the most expensive spa in the
area. For a good part of the night Ermengarda wandered about the house. She confabulated with her
parents, now my neighbors in the next apartment.
They must have been tired, for they had arrived that
afternoon from a long sight-seeing trip through Uru-
guay, Argentina, and Chile, made possible by their

daughter. (I did recognize her right to bother them until the wee hours of the morning.) She wandered through all the rooms and several times tried my door, repeating "Poly," "Poly," in a variety of tones ranging from affectionate to threatening. I spent a sleepless night listening and meditating. Taking advantage of the tranquillity that finally settled over the large house, I rose very early, locked Gran's ex-apartment, and took the key with me. I didn't even have breakfast. I grabbed my hat and my manuscript and went to the real estate agency. At ten o'clock Ermengarda phoned. Her voice was serene. She wanted to know if I could come home for lunch. Gran had arrived, blooming like a rose, and had asked for me. I needn't worry, she had given her the little blue room at the end of the hall and she was happy; the dear old thing was easily satisfied. It was a shame I couldn't come for lunch, there was turkey, but no matter, she would save me a piece of the breast meat and Gran could see me in the evening. I reflected that for the first time in many years I had had a civilized conversation with my wife.

In the club restaurant I read my "Eulogy to the São Paulo Lady" in a low voice to my secretary. She listened in silent concentration, from time to time making a gesture of approval. Her lengthy commentary indicated critical spirit and good taste. The theme I had chosen, she said, was more difficult than it seemed, principally because many people—hundreds, perhaps thousands—had already dealt with it. She herself had used it twice in compositions, in grade school and high school. Figures like the orator Ibrahim Nobre and the poet Guilherme de Almeida, besides other members of the São Paulo Academy of Letters, had already consecrated the topic in memorable

speeches and writings. Nevertheless, I had rejuvena-
ted the subject matter; in order to throw São Paulo
womanhood into relief, I had skillfully presented the
Paulista people not as Titans but rather as ordinary
folk pledged to efforts not always honorable, and vul-
nerable to fear like anyone else. Her last observation
surprised me, but I didn't argue; I had read that literary works are often subject to different interpreta-
tions, and that it was not the author's place to judge
them.

She concluded by saying that she was surprised to
learn that I dedicated myself to writing. She had noticed that my business letters were rewritten many
times, but she had thought that this was mere professional scruples. It was more than that; I was obviously
very well prepared. I confessed that I had only a bachelor's degree in literature. Her round little face was
thoughtful for a minute. Then she said that I was the
only man who always surprised her. I answered that I
was equally surprised with her knowledge of the
academy. With a simplicity that went straight to my
heart, she explained that her father had been the jani-
tor of the building. On days when musical parties
were held, he could get free tickets for his family.

The afternoon went well. My partner and I resolved
some problems created by a demagogic law about
rental fees that had provoked a dangerous withdrawal of capital. I went home in a euphoric mood,
and from the front yard I could already hear the notes
of an old waltz being played on the Bechstein grand
piano I had given Ermengarda as a wedding present,
assuming—wrongly—that she knew how to play. I
went into the living room and surprised Gran, whose
seventy-year-old fingers ran nimbly over the keys,
fingers which a month ago I had seen stiffened with

arthritis. I concluded that the disdain of modern medicine for mineral water cures was unfounded and
complimented the old lady. My enthusiasm for her
good health was sincere; a few weeks ago I had felt
some suspicious pains in the joints of my hands.
Ermengarda appeared smiling and asked in a low
voice that I give her the key to my apartment so the
maid could straighten up. The manner with which
she acknowledged my takeover was not polemic; she
had recognized a conquest. She had saved me a good
piece of turkey and dinner was pleasant. I went
straight up to my apartment where I reread the "Eulogy" and took the shower I had skipped in my morning's haste. Upon lying down, enveloped only by the
perfume of English lavender, I felt like a general: tired
but victorious.

My new situation gained with such ease, the success of my "Eulogy," and the fact that business was
going well gave me new confidence. I reread innumerable books from my military and political library
and followed the lesson of Caesar and Napoleon, employed later on by Rommel and Patton: don't worry
about solidifying acquired territory but keep advanc-
ing in order to confuse the enemy's calculations and
make it harder for him to operate. Like the German
asking Hitler for a free hand in Africa or the American
in Sicily untangling himself from the embarrassments
created by Eisenhower, I resolved that sex for me
would be free and untrammeled. I renounced the idea
of having children with Ermengarda and never gave
in to her acrid calls for intimacy in the sleepless nights
when I could hear her ghostlike, supplicating murmur on the other side of my door. This point resolved, I went on to the blockade. The government
edicts at that time were so confused that I had no

trouble convincing Ermengarda that the banks had canceled all current joint accounts, *and or.* She would have her personal account and every month the amount necessary for her expenses would be deposited. However, the very first month I restricted her funds drastically, with immediate results. The imported liquor served beside the pool was replaced by domestic; the good bottles in stock became reserved for consular personages. The supply ran out, though, and at the same time I reduced the numerous servants to one, whose exclusive job was taking care of the pool. The consuls of the United States and England were the first to go into eclipse, with the representatives of Paraguay, Ecuador, and other lesser powers following on their heels. The Brazilian snob sector accompanied the foreigners in the retreat, but there remained a nucleus of those faithful to Ermengarda —and to Brahma or Antarctica beer. In short, the more demanding rats abandoned us before the shipwreck. I never did like those people, and the proof is that I never even thought of doing any real estate business with any of them. Ermengarda had some distinguished contacts, high public functionaries from good São Paulo families, but they didn't frequent the pool.

Oriented by my political and military studies, I attentively watched her behavior after the bank account blow and often I admired her. I had a good appetite and her first maneuver was to make dinners extremely frugal. I imagined that she and her dear old people must gorge themselves at lunchtime, and discovered that she presided over clandestine suppers in the apartments of her guests. In doing this she could count on the faithfulness of the servants, whose salaries she constantly raised. I was in an ambivalent situation. I am a reserved person, and subordinates hardly ever appreciate my better qualities. Besides, I am sure she subtly turned the servants against me. During the time that I was deciding which side to take, I ate less at night and the insomnia that had infected me went away. I began to eat more at the agreeable luncheons with my secretary. I had never felt better.

Ermengarda's next assault was a sentimental one. Knowing my fondness for her arthritic grandmother, she asked if she should cancel the next session for Gran at Águas de São Pedro. I had prepared myself to confront any variation in the enemy's psychological offensive and, in answer, said no. My office would make the necessary arrangements. Gran would not go to the Grand Hotel, but she had a room reserved at Our Lady of the Annunciation Boardinghouse. The food at this boardinghouse left a little to be desired, which was actually an advantage; older people shouldn't eat much. I took advantage of Ermengarda's silence to enlarge upon this new theme; after a few theoretical observations, I alluded casually to the lunches and dinners which would eventually ruin the old peoples' health. Driven into a corner, the granddaughter of Gramps and Grams and daughter of Mom and Pop reacted with unexpected violence. Momentarily the old Ermengarda resurged in the new role of the outraged offspring defending her own. It was the last time she attacked me frontally. I was completely wrong if I thought that Hermengarda didn't see through everything, she screamed in tears. The whore I was having lunch with every day didn't fool Hermengarda with her disguise as the efficient and well-behaved little secretary. ''Yes, Dona Hermengarda. No, Dona Hermengarda. It's already been taken care of, Dona Hermengarda." *Hermengarda* pronounced over the phone by the secretary provoked such nausea in Ermengarda that she resolved never to call me again.

This affront to my secretary bothered me. The previous afternoon she had asked if I were still writing. I said no, without further comment. The truth was that all the energy I had left over from business affairs I channeled into the domestic battle or readings on political and military strategy. Her interest encouraged me to confide in her that I had reread the "Eulogy" and made a few changes. She wanted to know if I had typed the manuscript yet and offered to do it for me, asking permission to keep a copy. I had a few doubts; I didn't know if I should consider the text finished and wondered if perhaps the last part should be broadened in the final version to become a sort of peroration directed to the young womanhood of São Paulo which, thanks to her, I was now getting to know better. I explained the problem. Her honesty was complete: she hadn't thought about the subject, she liked the "Eulogy" just as it was, but perhaps I was right. After all, I was much more competent than she to judge and decide. We agreed that I would do the revision before giving her the first draft to be typed. I promised that I would do it right away, deciding to use the limited free time left me by business in the office and war at home. Ermengarda's defamation of this totally innocent young woman might have provoked open combat, for I had lost my fear. However, my head had gotten used to working detachedly since the beginning of the hostilities, and I demonstrated interest only in the allusion to the luncheons at the club. Evidently she had been spying on me. I soon discovered her agent, an old retired policeman. It was simple to gain the poor man's confidence. For having refused to mistreat prisoners, he had been relegated to an inferior position and had been ridiculed by his colleagues, some of whom later acquired such prestige that their names appeared in the foreign press. He added, with a touch of envy, that to abuse young men—and especially girls (he was the father of daughters) incapable of defending themselves—was against the solid upbringing for which his family had gone through sacrifice to give him. He had finished junior high school at the Liceu Nacional Rio Branco and had been taught morality and citizenship in the old manner by Professor Lourenço Filho. In spite of being poorly paid, he preferred to work for cuckolds and jealous women. I owe to this individual, so little favored by good fortune, the knowledge that there is no feminine form for *cuckold*.

On our second meeting the man was already complaining about the ridiculously low sum that he was getting to spy on me. I encouraged him to demand more, for I had observed that in spite of my restrictions, Ermengarda still had plenty of money at her disposal. According to my calculations she continued to spend, on the house and on her relatives, a sum far above what was in the bank account. Since even England censored mail during wartime, it was without scruples that I intercepted letters and discovered that my wife was still receiving the pension that her ex-husband had promised her on the condition of never again trying to contact him or their son. I put our spy in charge of verifying the amount, which was respectable considering the recession (happily temporary) then inflicting itself on the prosperity of São Paulo.

The spy, at least, couldn't complain about the economic crisis; paid now by me and by Ermengarda, and possibly also by the ex-husband, he could live in complete comfort without other clients. As for me, I wasn't any bother to him, since I didn't need to find out much about Ermengarda, trusting in my instincts and my theoretical experience in war and politics. I utilized him principally to furnish her with careful doses of information about me, some false, others true after the pattern of such operations. More than anything else I wanted to preserve my secretary's good name, and the informant must have told the truth about our relationship—that it was strictly professional in spite of the daily lunches together. I deliberately omitted our growing literary intimacy, which had nothing to do with it anyway. At the same time I charged him to invent and pass along information about adventures with imaginary women. I never had precise motives for complaints against our spy. If I dispensed with his services, it was to escape the dilemma which robs sleep from eminent officials of the world's most important countries: to know, in the last analysis, who is the party most favored by the activities of double or triple agents. What complicates the problem is that the agents themselves, when they are strictly mercenary, aren't able to say which person they help the most since they don't know the real implications of the information obtained. An episode with our spy demonstrates this aspect of the problem very well. He told me that a client—an old cuckold now separated from his wife—had ordered him to find out the ex-wife's exact age. Something told me that the client in question must be Ermengarda's ex-husband. The spy recalled this case to illustrate his theory about the pettiness of cuckolds, since according to him the rancorous fellow's only objective was to reveal his ex-wife's true age in the social circles they had frequented. This conversation of the old policeman's came up due to his client's interest in finding out the real age of my secretary. As for me, I told him that day to find out if Ermengarda still had other bank accounts unknown to me. The good man was impressed by the contrast between the seriousness of my preoccupations and the frivolity of the probable ex-husband's interests, as well as those of Dona Hermengarda herself. He said this in a respectful tone, aspirating the *H* as duly instructed by her. I believe he was mistaken on this point. The real motive of so-and-so's curiosity was undoubtedly to find out if his ex-wife had falsified the birth certificate she had presented in applying for her other papers: an eventual annulment of the marriage might be obtained through such proof. As for my secretary, she looked like an adolescent, which led Ermengarda to hope that she might be a minor. Since she was convinced we were lovers, she obviously was planning a scandal which would compromise my surname—widely known in the city's business circles—and who knows, maybe even my first name too.

There never was an armistice between us. However, in the manner of the old-fashioned trench wars, ours entered upon a period of stability which I used to reread political and military classics and brush up on postwar publications. Even so I found time to devote to my own writing. I put a lot of work into the ''Eulogy to the São Paulo Lady'' before showing the final version to my partner and my brothers. The former laughed—ever since we were adolescents he had made fun of my literary inclinations—but my dear brothers showed their usual supportiveness. My sec-

retary encouraged me in new undertakings. At home
the atmosphere was calmer. The swimming pool continued to be animated, but the old folks shortened
their visits. People of means, they owned houses in
Campinas, Jundiaí, and thereabouts, which were presented to them by their granddaughter and daughter
during her first marriage. These properties were numerous and appreciating fast, according to an already
out-of-date list from the spy. I mention these details
only to clarify why these old people, in excellent
health except for Gran and her arthritis, felt a dimin-
ishing attraction for a comfortable house where one
ate less and less all the time.

The household routine became as stagnant as
those phases of the First World War when Germans
and French, fifty yards apart in their respective
trenches, would look at each other absentmindedly
without firing a shot. I even began to sleep with the
door open; years before Ermengarda had given up
any resistance on this front. In spite of the absentminded way I followed my wife's movements, one
indisputably new fact aroused my curiosity: Ermengarda was writing. I don't refer to the letters,
which by now I didn't even bother to steam open
above the teakettle. It was a great notebook with a
purple cover that she constantly carried with her all
over the house, hugging it protectively to her breast
as if she were afraid someone would tear it away
from her by force. In the library, in the dining
room, even in the kitchen I often found her absorbed in her writing, pen in hand. As soon as she
saw me, she would quickly close the notebook and
go off with it. Depending on the light, the purple
cover would sometimes acquire a bluish tone. I
asked her without sarcasm if it was her account

book. She answered quite simply that it was something Hermengarda had been doing ever since she was a girl, just unimportant scribblings, a sort of diary, nonsense to make the time pass. I expressed surprise, since I had never before noticed this. She thought a minute before replying. She spoke in a mild tone and her ideas had an order of which I hadn't thought her capable. First, I never had paid much attention to what she did. Second, this notebook was larger than the one she normally used; Rosenheim's had gotten the order wrong and sent this one. She found it a bit inconvenient, but she liked the purple of the cover. Third, Hermengarda was writing more now than before. It helped her think. This observation corresponded to my experience with the "Eulogy." It had been a long time since I conversed with her, since I don't term as conversation the everyday exchange of words between man and wife. Hearing what she said about the notebook, I had the pleasant sensation that my wife was somebody else, but I didn't pursue the feeling.

One afternoon when I arrived home I found the notebook open on the table, the entire page full of her round and voluminous handwriting. I could hear her voice talking on the living room telephone. I lowered my eyes to the notebook absently but what I saw piqued my curiosity. Even as I tried to read what was written, I was obliged to follow the development of the phone conversation so as to foresee the instant she hung up. To get caught red-handed in such an indiscretion was contrary to my idea of elegant behavior. She was making an appointment with our dentist, but as he was one of the swimming pool crowd, the conversation was lengthy; I was able to read through the two pages and go directly up to my apartment as if I had just gotten home. In spite of the unfavorable conditions, the reading had greatly interested me. The diary hinted that Ermengarda felt attracted to some of the men who frequented the pool. Glimpsing a way out of a difficult situation that I had studied many times to no avail, my imagination began to work. I was dealing with the classic problem of a prolonged war during which the potential winner finds himself incapable of securing a decisive victory. I couldn't manage to see how Ermengarda's capitulation might come about, because at this juncture all the books in which I had studied historic precedents didn't help me at all. The domestic siege designed to reduce her to hunger and retreat to Jundiaí or Campinas was ineffective in the face of the ex-husband's subsidization. If Ermengarda were disposed to spend his money, the house and pool could return to their former glory for an indeterminate period of time. To expel her *manu militari* was against my upbringing, sentiments, principles, and style. An elegant gesture would be to leave her the house and go away; many times I had thought about doing just that but had always drawn back. In view of the crisis that my office and the business community in general feared, which could fall at any moment, the house represented a considerable investment, made more valuable by the modern wing where my convenient quarters were located. If worse came to worst the house could be transformed into a small, very high-class London-style hotel; they were lacking in our city. To surrender this stronghold would be a false victory; I couldn't pay that high a price for peace. What else could I hope for—Ermengarda's death? It was a hypothesis discarded at first glance. Her family's longevity had paraded before my eyes for years on end—and continued to do so. Probably there no longer existed in the entire state of São Paulo a mule gifted with a fatal kick. The dangers of the city? Ermengarda was careful, and back then serious accidents to pedestrians were rare.

Up to that time it had not occurred to me that Ermengarda might be capable of loving anyone who did not contribute in a direct way to her existence. But now I saw a solution: she would fall in love, go away, and lose the war, the house, and me. There were three admirers she found alluring. Their names, or rather their abbreviations, were registered in the purple notebook: Alf, Dec, and Cincin. I find it very hard to memorize abbreviations or initials; they seem harder to me than full names, and the swimming pool nomenclature had always baffled me. What faces, what half-naked bodies might be concealed behind those letters? Dec and Cincin meant nothing to me. Alf might be the big happy American, the only one from the consulate who hadn't accompanied his colleagues in the desertion. They said he was a secret agent overseeing the control of São Paulo bigwigs, beginning with the governor. Absurd to imagine that he would come to our house to spy on Ermengarda or myself. My youthful enthusiasm for integralism had given way to purely Paulista sentiments, less spectacular but solid. The man must be after my wife.

The next morning I spent hours in the pool. The disappointments piled up one on top of the other. The American was called Robert, Rob; Alf was only Alfredinho; and Dec was Pradinho, whose first name I hadn't realized was Decio. Alf and Dec were

Ermengarda's godsons. I didn't deny that they were attractive young men, but it was obvious they were in no condition to make my wife abandon her home, which was essential. The legislation protecting common-law wives, one of the immoral initiatives taken by President Getúlio Vargas, stipulated continuous cohabitation. The minute Ermengarda left home to accompany another man she would lose the right to financial compensation or inheritance, even if she came back repentant the next day and her cohabitant took her in out of pity. The important thing was to witness and register everything. Obviously, the two young fellows wouldn't do. No judge would take them seriously, unless they went into his own house to seduce his wife, daughters, or housemaid. That left Cincin. This was the biggest surprise of all: he was Dr. Cincinato, our dentist, a sordid miser but a competent professional. He earned wads of money in the consulting room installed in his shabby house in São Bento Street near the Praça do Patriarca. He didn't even have an assistant to fasten the napkin around his clients' necks. In spite of Ermengarda's lack of interest in water, I couldn't imagine her living in that hovel. Still, with the American dream lost, Cincin was the most plausible of the three. To my wife's astonishment I invited the dentist to dinner. Her alarm increased when she saw me arrive early, bringing reinforcements of food wrapped in paper from Casa Godinho. Cincinato was already there, which seemed a good omen. The dinner went well, although naturally he was restless and constrained. As for Ermengarda's coolness toward our guest, it could only be dissimulation. On the pretext of finishing an urgent bit of work, I excused myself after the coffee, saying I must be absent for a few minutes. I went to the library and left them at their ease. I reread my "Eulogy" and decided that it still needed a few small modifications, such as substituting the adjective *red* for *scarlet* and using a colon instead of a semicolon in the last sentence. I would consult my secretary the next day. When I went downstairs three-quarters of an hour later, Cincinato had left and Ermengarda was writing. I hung about hoping to observe something new, but it was useless. Ermengarda went on writing until late without minding my presence, which had never happened before. From time to time she unconsciously corrected the position of the notebook, raising it so that the purple of the cover acquired its curious bluish tone in the lamplight. She interrupted her writing only to say that she had finally found something to do in her sleepless nights. I went to bed convinced that in order to assure the effectiveness of my next moves it was indispensable that I read the purple notebook. The following morning, Ermengarda complained about her teeth and about Dr. Cincinato. He had never fixed up his office and his treatments were painful. To my despair she announced she was going to find another dentist. It was ever more urgent to read what she wrote, but then the occasion presented itself spontaneously. One afternoon I didn't find Ermengarda in the living room where she customarily waited for me. After some time had passed I went up to her room, expecting to find her sick, since I had noticed she was a bit pallid that morning. I knocked. Nobody answered, so I opened the door. The first thing I saw was the notebook on her dressing table, its purple tone altered by some traces of face powder. Fearing an ambush, I closed the door and called her name in a loud voice. The butler appeared to say that Madame had gone to Jundiaí to visit her father, who had a cold, and would not be back until the next day. She had taken the Chrysler. If I needed the Buick, the keys were in her room, in the dressing-table drawer.

I spent the night reading and rereading the purple notebook. From a literary standpoint it was mediocre; the vocabulary was poor, there were elementary diction errors and even mistakes of grammatical agreement. But never did a piece of writing impress me more, in spite of my having read the best Portuguese authors and several French ones in the original when I was younger. The memoirs of generals and politicians don't count, since they aren't meant to be literature.

The feeling that Hermengarda was another person once more dominated my reading and crept into my long meditations. She didn't permit me to forget the Ermengarda of my immediate personal experience, since she wrote in the third person and constantly inscribed her name with a voluminous *H*. Still, discounting these nervous habits (innocent, after all) I recognized her only faintly. Places, persons, and scenes totally familiar to me—even I myself—acquired a completely original meaning in the purple notebook. The narratives, some of them long and detailed, were far from being the scribbles and notations to which she had modestly referred when she spoke to me of her writing. This was a genuine, intimate diary, lived through and suffered, literarily inept but for that very reason authentic and full of emotion. The first suspicion invoked by the reading was that Hermengarda loved me. This hunch was prompted by the last few pages where I had begun to read. They referred to Cincin, Alf, and Dec. The two young men had given her a heavy rush, to which she had responded with maternal condescension, avoiding their humiliation even as she confessed how flattered she was. She handled the situation with such poise and candor that the young fellows ended up being amused at the absurdity of their pretensions and made her their confidante in matters of the heart. With Cincin things weren't so simple. He was a mature and sour man on the brink of old age, seeking some exciting compensation for a stagnant life spent in the company of gaping-mouthed clients or in the isolation of his dingy, mean quarters. The mornings by the pool, the smiles flashing with teeth he had no obligation to examine, opened new vistas for him, and he dreamed they might involve my wife. Patient and understanding, Hermengarda made a few moves which, wrongly interpreted, could have compromised her. Dr. Cincinato really was losing his head. If she called to make an appointment, he would cancel all his previous engagements without the slightest concern, which was odd. The clients found these repeated postponements an abuse and they deserted him. My wife would consent to move from the dental chair equipped with an old-fashioned cuspidor to a threadbare seat in the waiting room where she would listen, glass of soda-pop in hand, to Cincin's endless declarations of love. Out of kindness, she tried patiently to reason with him. However, it wasn't possible to reach a modus vivendi similar to that which had enriched the lives of the boys. The dentist became demanding, and Hermengarda saw that she had no choice but to renounce the friendship; in fact, she thought she should have done so sooner.

Among the motives she enumerates to justify her imprudence, one touched me to the quick: although writing only for herself, she blushes at her own childishness in imagining that by prolonging her friend-

ship with Cincin she could—who knows—cause me to
wonder, make me care for her again. I here transcribe
her thought in the same terms her modesty selects,
but it seems clear to me that instead of *wonder* she
should have *grow jealous* and where she writes *care for*
one should read *love.* Reading the whole of the purple
notebook not only confirmed my first impressions,
but also constituted dramatic proof (in spite of its indi-
rect and discreet mode of expression) that Hermengarda's love for me not only existed but was un-
changed. I'm explaining it badly: it wasn't only the
Hermengarda of the intimate diary who emerged as
another woman; I also emerged as another man. She
describes me respectfully, using only my habitual surname known to everyone in the office, the club, and
the city. It was necessary for me to read the diary to
realize that Hermengarda had stopped calling me
Poly a long time ago. That explained why, at a time
difficult to pin down precisely, I had begun circulat-
ing carelessly about the pool far from Ermengarda's
vocal cords. I had then experienced a state of inner
comfort, which I interpreted as self-awareness and as-
sertion of my own personality. Actually, I owed it to
Hermengarda. This and other examples of the traps
laid by subjectivity, all illustrated in the diary, deeply
impressed me. Another story she relates, along with
my thoughts about it, attests to the importance of
these revelations, through which we discover our
emotional inadequacy to comprehend even the sim-
plest realities. After she began to sleep alone, Hermengarda's insomnia got worse. A doctor advised
her to soak in a warm bath just before bedtime, using
eucalyptus-scented soap. The results were excellent
and Hermengarda never again failed to follow this
routine. Now the curious thing is this. In the course of

these same years I would sit down twice a day at the same table with Hermengarda, for breakfast and dinner. On birthdays we exchanged embraces. Yet, during all that time I continued to notice the characteristic odor, although it had, of logical necessity, disappeared. On summer mornings when the windows were thrown wide, I had occasionally sniffed the agreeable fragrance of eucalyptus, which I ascribed to the trees in the garden, where in fact there were none. This means that I had before my eyes a real Hermengarda whom I didn't perceive, didn't see, didn't even smell because I had substituted for her another woman cultivated by my imagination. Parallel to this, my own personality re-created in the purple notebook, though clearly corresponding to that which I tried to present to others, really had nothing to do with the personality that existed inside me. I've already mentioned the respect she expressed for me in her diary. Her accounts of our fights are interspersed with tough self-criticisms for her ineptitude in expressing herself, lack of tact, and wild polemics. Contrasted to her verbal excess was my silence, which she interpreted as an effort at understanding and compliance, remarking on it at length and with praise. Her notebook portrayed me as purehearted, incapable of mistrust or lies, yet at the same time proud and noble. Reading these sections I felt my face burn with shame; her praise stripped unbearably naked all that was sly, calculating, and cruel in me.

I was particularly moved by the various passages in which Hermengarda goes back to the scene involving the "Eulogy to the São Paulo Lady." One sees that she had difficulty in recounting it, for several times she abandons it as if the memory were too painful. When I skimmed over the diary the

first time I naturally assumed that my wife's unhappiness was due to the fight caused by my insistence that I read her the "Eulogy." However, it became clear that Hermengarda did not remember the
exact moment of the incident at all; she did not establish any link between her reaction and my subse-
quent behavior, starting with my abandonment of
our old bedroom. The text lacked temporal aware-
ness, describing and commenting on facts that were
often years apart. The episodes themselves, completely disconnected, were what had pricked her
memory. Apparently she was convinced I hadn't
given the "Eulogy" scene the slightest importance.
When she finally managed to narrate it in a continuous manner, she did so with a fluency and quality
of emotion that was nowhere else repeated. The beginning of my "Eulogy" impressed her vividly. Although confessing that she was ignorant, she also
recognized that she was discovering a new dimension in me. I understood this more clearly as I recalled that the introduction to my little work is quite
general; only in the second stanza does it present
historical examples. Hermengarda had followed
my reading in fascination up to the moment when
she realized that the poem dealt principally with
the role of the Paulista woman in 1932. At this
point, a wave of atrocious memories invaded her
mind and she can't remember what she said or did.
The only thing that remained clear was her an-
guished reaction to people who had unjustly hu-
miliated her in the past.

Hermengarda admirably relates the painful recol-
lections of her childhood in Campinas. It was during
the Constitutionalist Revolution. Politicians and important military figures had gone to the Campinas

schools to make speeches and work in the "Gold for Victory" campaign. Even the children were mobilized to go from house to house gathering coins and rings so that São Paulo could pay for planes and weapons to guarantee the invincibility of our troops. The teacher maliciously gave Hermengarda the special task of visiting her neighbor, an old Italian telegraphist. His grandson was her best friend among the neighborhood children, and the adults called them the "little sweethearts." The old man received Hermengarda affectionately and laughed hard when he heard her request. Speaking with a friend who was present, he said it was too late, São Paulo's goose was cooked and served already, *enfarinato*. What the teachers should do was to make the children study instead of filling their hollow little heads with the tomfoolery of deranged politicians and soldiers whose absurd revolution was doomed to failure. Hermengarda thought the opinion of her little friend's grandfather very strange but she conscientiously carried out her mission. At school, her report was the one most anxiously awaited. She began to speak in the silence of the crowded classroom. The news that the old man refused to trade his widower's wedding ring for the patriotic ones of zinc was received with a disapproving murmur that became an indignant roar as she related with total innocence the part about São Paulo's goose being cooked and served *enfarinato*. The poor little girl sensed that the catcalls and boos were aimed at her as well, but she didn't understand why. The teacher asked her severely what she intended to do from now on, but little Hermengarda didn't say a word, not comprehending. The intrepid schoolmarm repeated her attack, demanding whether Hermengarda would set foot in the house of the telegraphist again. Trying to alleviate the hostile atmosphere, Hermengarda said she would do whatever the teacher ordered. The latter smiled unsympathetically and pressed her to say whether she intended to continue playing with her "little sweetheart" or not. Another murmur rose in the classroom as though the booing might start again. The poor little defendant wanted to cry at this unexpected question and tried to muffle her sobs as she nodded yes, red as a beet. The booing was terrible, but the headmistress imposed order, and the teacher was able to deliver an exalted speech of accusation against the entire family of the old telegraph operator. They were known supporters of the dictatorship, named for fat jobs by the dictator's puppet in São Paulo, Colonel Manuel Rabelo, "the friend of the beggars," she emphasized sarcastically. These "beggars" were downtrodden Northeasterners or foreigners whom the generous Paulista heart had charitably received. And now they were spitting the filth of betrayal into the very plate that nourished them. They held positions of responsibility; one was in the tax office, another in the Prefecture, a third in the office of the municipal court, not to mention the oldest brother who sold coffee in the police headquarters, which explained the immunity they all enjoyed. The worst was the telegraphist who, besides being a foreigner, a dictator-lover, and an anarchist, spent his nights listening to the radio from Rio de Janeiro and his days spreading the enemy's rumors about the city.

The *Campinas Sentinel* gave front-page coverage to the school assembly, carrying the principal parts of the speech, including the girl's information that São Paulo's goose was cooked. The family of my future wife kept a copy of the paper which Hermengarda, now a young girl, read over many times in tears. The

only detail omitted by the reporter was the final answer Hermengarda gave at the end of the meeting.
Pressured by the headmistress to declare loyally in
front of everyone what she was going to do from now
on, the exhausted girl limited herself to saying that
she intended to continue playing with the neighbor
boy. Her schoolmates turned their backs on her the
next day and the teacher asked her parents to remove
her from school. In spite of their alarm at the impris-
onment of the old telegraphist and the coffee vendor
at the police station, Hermengarda's parents per-
mitted the children to go on seeing each other, but
only in the backyard so as not to suffer embarrassments from the more exalted old ladies, the ones who
hunted for victims to torture. By the middle of Sep-
tember the children were able to go back to playing
hopscotch on the sidewalk; the army from Minas
Gerais was moving closer to Campinas and the old
ladies were in the churches begging for peace at any
price.

The chapter about Hermengarda's childhood in
Campinas occupied a good part of the notebook, with
richly detailed anecdotes indicating the vulnerability
of her small being. The school ordeal stayed with her
but perhaps would have faded if it hadn't been for a
highly unpleasant incident during her first marriage.
Her sisters-in-law, active members of the Paulista Association for Feminine Action (PAFA), an organiza-
tion formed to defend society against the breakdown
of tradition, thought it strange that she shouldn't be a
contributing member of their body. They asked,
alluding to Hermengarda's Northeastern and South-
ern background, if she didn't now feel sufficiently
Paulista to join—this in spite of her being native to
Jundiaí. To make them happy, Hermengarda filled

out the forms: born in Jundiaí, educated in Campinas, married in São Paulo, one son who was still a baby. The subject was forgotten until the day one of the sisters-in-law, her eyes hard and shining, announced that Hermengarda's petition for membership had been refused. Perplexed, Hermengarda appealed in vain to her husband's sisters, who politely excused themselves; they knew only about the refusal of membership, that was all. As a last try, Hermengarda went to the PAFA office. The president could not find time to see her, but a law student, secretary of the association, politely explained to her that the files of the PAFA were strictly confidential and unfortunately he couldn't do anything for her. Fortunately, he could. Hermengarda bribed him and got hold of a copy of the voluminous file bearing her name. The greater part of it consisted of information furnished by the Campinas chapter of the PAFA. When she read the name of the local chapter president, everything at once became clear. This person was an enemy of her family's; a woman whose animosity had begun long before Hermengarda's birth. The shrew had publicly accused Gran of being mistress to her husband, a handsome young man who was a gambler and a bohemian, but good at heart. Unconcerned about his bad reputation, Gran had tried to help him by introducing him to Padre Crispim, thus creating the rumors that led to the woman's slanderous remarks. The woman was an incredibly ugly hag who would never have managed to marry the grandson of noblemen if it hadn't been for her money. Reading the name of the informer who had sent the São Paulo chapter the "complete data—objective and impartial—about the party in question," Hermengara was surprised that the busybody was still alive, since she was even older than Gran.

Gran was further enraged as she realized that the Campinas chapter of PAFA had added a considerable number of years to her age in order to make their calumny look true. They presented her as having been an adolescent in '32, an almost-grown woman who refused to serve as a nurse, sabotaged the ''Gold for Victory'' campaign, and jeered at the war effort. She lived hidden in the forests with a young telegraph operator, probably her lover, imprisoned due to his manifest sympathy for the regime. The account followed Hermengarda's life up to her moving to São Paulo, but apart from a few hints about other male company it didn't add anything else. It wound up with general information about her family, established in Campinas for three generations. Nevertheless, they weren't of Campinas or even Paulista stock. The men were considered hard workers and the wives good housekeepers, but among the older women there were those who did not excel in decorum. The slur on Gran came just before the enormous signature of the president. She read it all and was deeply hurt, but scorned this infamy that was to have such grave consequences for her health. From that time on she was constantly traumatized by the simple association between São Paulo women and the Revolution of 1932. Whenever this connection came up—ever more rarely with the persistent progress of Brazil—she would fall into a morbid depression that worried the doctors. The PAFA's denunciation also had more immediate effects on her life. Her sisters-in-law stopped seeing her. Hermengarda's brother, although he was extremely loyal, gradually let his mind be poisoned. The solution was to separate. Hermen-

garda firmly insists that this was one of the best
moves she ever made in a life full of vexations and
suffering.

Next there appeared a nebulous phrase, repeated
and rewritten many times, in which Hermengarda
seemed to confess that she could accept the sacrifice
of her son when she considered the thing destiny had
reserved for her in exchange. I reread these lines carefully before I came to the poignant theory that *the
thing* might be myself. As the night passed and I read
it over and over again, the purple notebook became
an inexhaustible source of information. One part, for
example, to which I paid the attention due it only on
the fourth or fifth reading, took on crucial significance. It refers to the fairness with which Hermengarda viewed her husband's devotion to his sisters,
although it was responsible for a very serious crisis in
her life. The light of understanding was shed on her
behavior toward my brothers in keeping them away
from our house. Unconsciously she saw a genuine
danger in their fraternal love for me, this time incomparably graver than that which threatened her first
marriage. The notebook didn't mention my partner's
disloyalty, nor did it need to. I could see everything as
the blindfold dropped from my eyes. Why had he listened to me read the "Eulogy to the São Paulo Lady"
with a sardonic air and then not said a word? Even I
had never thought my first literary effort so important; it would have been much more loyal of him to
say frankly what he thought, like a true friend, instead of laughing at me.

All my prejudices against Hermengarda, caused by
the complete distortion of reality in which I had been
lost, were obliterated by the purple notebook—even
those that seemed the most obvious and were thus

the most deceiving. The need to speak and hear her own name continually, which I had put down to simple narcissism, were actually rooted in her early difficulty to communicate with herself and others. The diary is replete with vivid childhood remembrances. Even when she grew into early adolescence she was unable to say her own name correctly. To help her with this delicate problem her parents, advised by a psychologist from the university, suggested that those around her call her always by name, and that the child do the same when she spoke of herself. Thanks to this technique her mental development was stabilized as she grew to adulthood. It maintained her psychological balance so well that Hermengarda could not do without the aid of her name—it had become part of the foundation of her personality. Following the case closely, the psychologist advised that no one should interfere with this verbalization, which at once reflected and resolved the serious problem of auto-identification, one of the greatest problems faced by psychology. In the same context, Hermengarda also had trouble with the memorization and classification of other peoples' names. She overcame this on her own, by inventing a system of abbreviations. The way others became aware of the girl's invention is deliciously picturesque. She was back in school. Her proficiency in arithmetic had blossomed, but she was making no progress in history or geography. Then suddenly she became first in her class in these subjects as well. But her parents were disturbed because, instead of preparing her lessons at the little white desk she had been given, she spent hours in the backyard with a paper in her hand, reciting strange words like Amacapima, Parcabel, Pedalca, Dudecax, Flopeixo, etc. . . . until they discovered, delighted,

what these names stood for: Amazonas, capital
Manaus; Pará, capital Belém; Pedro Alvares Cabral;
Duque de Caxias; Floriano Peixoto, and so on.

The happiness caused me by the purple notebook
was tarnished by a sudden apprehension rising from
the last few pages. Hermengarda again mentions her
insomnia; the evening baths with eucalyptus soap no
longer had any effect. Her inability to sleep was due
to anxiety; she couldn't rest because she was suffering, and I was the cause. In a desperate effort to sleep
and forget, she was taking ever-larger doses of sleeping pills, against the doctor's dire warnings. Even
with the pills she only fell into a measured torpor assaulted by fear. She was afraid she might die riddled
with guilt at not having been the wife I deserved in
the short span of fifteen years—short when compared
to the eternity of her sentiments. She asked gloomily
if it weren't too late, and if the best solution wouldn't
indeed be her death. At least then I would be free to—
who knows?—start my life over, which she ardently
desired. Yet a voice from her deepest soul kept saying
that Hermengarda was the wife and companion that
destiny had chosen for me. If everything crumbled,
she, Hermengarda, would be the most to blame.

The last few lines of the diary spoke of her immediate departure for Jundiaí; she had just received news
from there. She would take advantage of the visit to
her sick father in order to seek inspiration from the
God of her childhood in the amiable setting of the city
that had cradled her. Depending on what she felt, she
would make a decision when she came back. There
was not one time during the whole night that I didn't
pause from reading the diary with my eyes swimming, but now, as morning dawned, I was sobbing,
crushed by emotion and fatigue, dying for Hermen-

garda to return that very instant and find forever the inseparable, insuperable companion of her life and insomnia.

The exhilaration that possessed me made rest impossible. Overcoming my fatigue with fresh new energy, I resolved to start the first day of the new era at once. Symbolically renewing my life together with Hermengarda I took a bath in her suite, now rubbing my muscles vigorously with eucalyptus soap, now caressing at length my intimate parts drowned in lather. In spite of the early hour, I tried to call Jundiaí, but to no avail. Thinking it might be easier to call from my office, I left without having anything to eat at that hour when the servants were just waking up. I gave orders to the butler that no one was to enter Madame's bedroom. I examined the notebook once more to make sure that handling it all night hadn't left marks on it, put it back in the same place I'd found it, and whitened its upper edge with a light dusting of face powder. I trembled at the idea of offending her if she discovered my indiscretion and realized that her secrets had been violated.

I spent the entire morning keeping the office telephone operator busy. The lines to Jundiaí were always "in use" or "interrupted," depending on the phrase that occurred to those in charge at the moment. I didn't take care of any business and kept my partner from doing so, since I didn't give him one chance at the telephone. (We didn't receive clients in the morning, so the phone was the office's lifeline.) About eleven my partner got impatient and came to talk to me. My answer must have made it clear that the major portion of the company belonged to me and that I was the boss. I couldn't find time or energy to see my brothers who arrived punctually—they routinely visited on Mondays and Thursdays—and I paid no attention to the secretary who spent the morning waiting for me to summon her. That day I didn't need her for anything, and I was irritated when I saw her arrive at the club as I mechanically began my lunch, absorbed in my thoughts. I decided that when an opportune moment arose I would point out to her the impropriety of sitting down at the boss's table without being invited. She found me worried; I found her indiscreet. Decidedly that girl was forgetting her place. She ate a few bites in silence and then remembered to make some remark about the ''Eulogy to the São Paulo Lady,'' which she said she had reread the night before. I didn't let her finish. I was annoyed with her insistent interruption of my thoughts and told her that I considered the ''Eulogy'' something bygone—or not even that, since ''bygone'' implied that it had once had some meaning, which wasn't the case. It was simply an insignificant exercise and even if she wished to show interest in this limited area, nobody besides myself would give her any acknowledgment for it. I arrested her reproving gesture with one of my own and continued. There was no point in discussing the poem's content, it had no importance in exercises of this type. I stopped, noting obliquely the girl's astonished eyes, in which I sensed a deceiving character, and realized to my satisfaction that certain ideas about the ''Eulogy'' had become clear to me. Resuming my speech, I told her that I had stopped thinking about the poem completely, to the point of forgetting to ask her for the copy she had typed. And without pausing I sent her back to the office to get busy with the correspondence. Alone at last, I signaled for the maître d' and asked him to get me a phone connection to Jundiaí. It was useless. When

I went back to the office I found the outer room crowded with clients, but within, work had been exchanged for the expectancy I saw stamped on every face. I asked about my partner; he had gone out and wasn't expected back. So much the better, I thought. I told the clients to come back another day and dismissed everyone except the phone operator. We spent the afternoon trying to reach Jundiaí. Finally I gave up; by this time Hermengarda would already be on her way back. I went home to wait for her. The big house in Alto dos Pinheiros was a tranquil oasis after the agitation of the office. But disappointment awaited me. Hermengarda had phoned from Campinas. She had extended her trip to stop briefly at Gran's, had asked if I was well, and said she would be back the next day.

My first reaction was despair. Gran didn't have a phone. As for a telegram, it was unthinkable. And how could I send a telegram if I didn't know the address? I didn't even know Gran's last name—nor her first name either, for that matter. Gran was the abbreviation of what? Of Grandmother, of course, I remembered with relief. I experienced a moment of panic as Gran dissolved into unreality and Hermengarda threatened to follow her, with me unable to find the slightest support or confirmation of Gran's existence beyond the echo of the sound produced by the four letters. Quickly I got back on course to avoid further risks. Gran was grandmother, Hermengarda's grandmother, her maternal grandmother, her mother's mother; her husband was a handsome young man who gambled—no, that was somebody else, her husband was a very hardworking fellow who had died in the flower of his youth, poor thing, of a mule kick. Hermengarda never—no, what nonsense—Gran never forgot him; she lives in Campinas, I know her very well, a charming old lady who suffers from arthritis; she goes to Águas de São Pedro for cures; she plays the piano, I like Gran tremendously. This momentary crisis past, I felt a great peace. Hermengarda had asked about me and would return tomorrow. I went up to her room where everything was as I had left it. I needed to exert willpower so as not to reopen the purple notebook. I feared I would be unable to leave it alone during the night and I wanted to be rested and ready for Hermengarda the next day. I wouldn't go to the office at all. She hadn't said what time she would be back, but it didn't matter, I would wait all day if need be, standing at the gate. A few seconds before I fell asleep I had a small auditory hallucination that made me open my eyes and smile: suspended in air, Hermengarda's voice murmured Poly, Poly.

I slept for ten hours and woke in the middle of the morning, startled by someone knocking on the door. It was a call from my office, the tenth. The butler had resisted the first nine, saying I was asleep and he had not been authorized to wake me. He capitulated when they told him that the situation was very grave, a question of the life and death of the firm. They requested that I go there immediately. I asked about my partner. He wasn't there, hadn't been in, but he had left an urgent letter for me. When I arrived at the office there was general confusion. Creditors, bank people, clients, suppliers, and nobody to make a decision. Diligently the secretary and the accountant had spoken to some of them, justifying, apologizing, trying to put things right. They seemed to be getting somewhere, and I was happy to see the secretary functioning efficiently, even at a distance. I forgave her impertinence of the day before. From time to time I rang home. No, Dona Hermengarda had not arrived. Phone busy, the crackle of a defective line, wrong number, lines crossed. When I got the right connection, I heard the implacable response: Dona Hermengarda had not yet arrived.

My partner's letter was laconic: he asked that I choose a lawyer in whom I had confidence to dissolve our association. He could be reached at such-and-such an address. My face angry and my thoughts bitter, I reflected that the hour of truth was at hand. Rancor, summed up in the disorder of the office, made me forget Hermengarda temporarily, which had not happened for two nights and a day. The news of my partner's resignation spread through the business community; the phone rang incessantly, the banks being anxious about the outcome of our current deals. I had no more time to think until the middle of the afternoon. Hungry, I ordered some sandwiches and called home one more time. The butler answered. Hermengarda had arrived! She had tried to call me several times, but the busy signal had convinced her that the line was out of order. At the moment she was resting a little; she had got home very tired, the butler concluded. I gave him strict orders not to let the servants disturb her; he should avoid the slightest noise. No floor buffers, no blenders, no vacuum cleaners, and above all he should turn off the little radio in the kitchen, a precursor to the abominable portable transistors that were to become an inseparable accessory of maids, a new sound-producing device that announced their presence as they went about the house. No one was to talk loudly; they should whisper among themselves only what was indispensable, and very softly, very softly. I particularly cautioned the butler, remembering that he had a rather loud voice. They should disconnect the phone and the doorbell, and station somebody in front of the house to attend to the vegetable man or other vendors who might appear to keep them from clapping their hands or shouting to advertise their goods, as vendors did in those days. I especially feared the baritone voice of the grape seller. "Marengo grapes, see the white graa-pes . . . gra-apes!" . . . with the interminable sonorous pauses. Nothing could be done about the bus, but fortunately our house was well back from the street. The neighborhood was calm, possibly nothing would interrupt the well-deserved rest of my Hermengarda. On my way to Alto dos Pinheiros I imagined, anxious and happy, how hard the two nights in Jundiaí and Campinas must have been for her. People subject to insomnia suffer a great deal when they travel; many things bother them in the strange nocturnal environment: the creaking of the house, the dimensions of the room and bed, the material of the pillowcase, and above all, the pillow. The only thing more important than the pillow was the person sharing the bed, who might sleep snuggled close or slightly apart, stretched out or curled up, belly down or sideways, facing in or turned away; whose figure might be parallel to the ceiling, nose pointing up, or in any of the infinite variety of diagonal positions as it lightly came in contact with the other's body.

The tomblike silence of the house pleased me. I went up the stairway on tiptoe and pressed my ear to the door. Still only silence. I would wait for her to wake up but I just wanted to look at her. I carefully opened the door a crack and saw three things: the notebook, the small empty bottle, and her grayish face. The doctor attested to the fact that she had been dead for about five hours.

The arrangements for Hermengarda's funeral gave me no trouble. Her relatives took charge of everything, sensibly preventing any news from reaching the old people in Jundiaí and Campinas and upsetting them. Later they would be told, and could come to the mass held after thirty days. The seventh-day mass, like the wake and funeral, took place in the strictest privacy; even my brothers and their wives were excluded. It was attended only by those members of her family who lived in the city of São Paulo, her godsons Alf and Dec, a few friends from the swimming pool crowd—among whom was poor Cincinato—and me. Nobody thought it strange that I should be unaccompanied; they were used to seeing me alone in my house and didn't know I had friends or brothers. In fact, I never really did. The secretary and the accountant, the only people from my office to whom I communicated the news of her death, limited themselves to a quick visit of condolence in keeping with my instructions. I took advantage of their coming to give them power of attorney so they could continue with business. I told them to take care of everything, I didn't know when I would be back at work.

Her suicide caught me psychologically unprepared in spite of the clarity of the last few pages that had made me weep during the long vigil of the purple notebook. I didn't know how to suffer, and sensing that the learning period would be long, I was in no hurry. While I waited for the pain to begin, I made the first preparations for my worship of Hermengarda's memory. I gave up trying to figure out the meaning of what she had scrawled shakily inside the back cover of the notebook with enormous handwriting announcing what she had just done. In the last line she hoped that Poly . . . and that was all. The effect of the drug had been quicker than her hand. I had ahead of me many years of expiation to do everything Hermengarda had hoped of me. I had already given orders at the office for Gran to be sent to the Grand Hotel again for her next cure. I chose some of Hermengarda's most characteristic possessions: a lipstick, a handkerchief with an elongated *H* embroidered on it, a loose key, a change of underclothes, and a half-used bar of eucalyptus soap. Methodically I went through all the dressers and cupboards, setting aside here a dress, there an umbrella, a pair of imitation gold earrings (the jewels I would offer to the ladies of the family), a fan, and some pretty shoes. A large locked drawer filled me with expectation. When I opened it with a key I found in her purse, my hopes rose: it was practically full of used-up notebooks. I recognized her handwriting at a glance. The treasure had been discovered—it was Hermengarda's complete diary! I decided to wait until nightfall to begin my reading, and put the relic away in the library safe. I wished to prepare myself spiritually for hours, weeks, years of the highest emotion.

The disappointment caused me by the material was enormous. The whole thing was basically a rough draft of what I had read in the purple notebook; there was not a single new element in the hundreds of pages I read. They showed only the insane task she had assigned herself in order to achieve the merely passable pages of the purple diary. The childhood sketch of Campinas in 1932, for example, had taken five entire exercise books. I read only the first one, formless and confused; the characters were so mixed up that even I, knowing the episode perfectly well, got lost trying to remember who was who. After they had revealed Hermengarda's exemplary determination to learn to write fluently, the practice notebooks were simply tiresome. I came quickly to the last of the pile, a big spiral tablet just like the purple one but with a blue cover. I was about to put it together with the others when I opened it in the middle by chance, and my eyes fell on a line where, near Cincin's name, there was a reference to the eucalyptus soap. I read the passage and learned that the baths had been suggested by Cincinato. I found this odd, since the purple notebook had left me with the impression that it was a doctor who had advised her and not a simple dentist. I thought about checking on this but I didn't have a chance. As I moved my head, my glance fell on a sentence whose last word hit me like a blow: "Only a cook old like Polydoro." The shock made me clench my eyes shut. Never had the execrable name assaulted me so treacherously. In the purple notebook Hermengarda hadn't even written Poly, the abbreviation which had lost its threatening power ever since I had heard her voice repeating it tenderly in that pleasant dream. And now she wrote the whole name out. But why? The hope that I had misread it came to me; the sentence seemed meaningless. I opened my eyes and looked directly at the last word. No doubt about it, the name was there intact with all its letters, not the carefully written ones of the purple diary but smaller and run together, yet indisputably hers. I reread the sentence and discovered why it was hard to understand. I had read "cook old," in her uneven hand, as two words instead of one. What she had actually written was "cuckold"—"Only a cuckold like Polydoro."

I resolved not to panic. I closed the notebook and

waited a moment. I opened it again with my head absolutely cool and read almost two hundred pages of tiny handwriting. The last few pages were blank. I didn't let a single illegibly written word escape without clarifying it. When I didn't understand a complicated sentence or passage, I went back and read it over until I made sense of it. This happened quite frequently because the blue notebook, unlike the purple one, was written in a very poor hand. It was obvious that she had written it only for herself, thus revealing for whom the other one had been so painstakingly prepared. I am not making a conjecture here; the truth was on every page and the actual reason for the existence of the blue notebook was to plan, filter, and comment on everything that would be put in the purple one—for me to read. The number of things I learned was prodigious. Cincinato had in fact recommended the eucalyptus baths, and the advice was anything but disinterested, because for months he had been Ermengarda's lover. Unlike the purple notebook, the blue one offered a controlled and exact chronology. The affair with the dentist began in the middle of April, during some orthodontal bridgework she had had done, which had seemed extremely expensive when I got the bill. They continued to meet until the day Cincinato came to dinner at my invitation. They had quarreled before I arrived, after having slept together one last time. Ermengarda had practically thrown him out of bed when he asked her for a fat sum to modernize his consulting room. She became indignant, thinking the dentist wanted to act the part of a gigolo. In my opinion, Dr. Cincinato would be incapable of that sort of thing, such a competent professional is he, a man full of merit, arriving here from his native state of Sergipe with nothing and

succeeding thanks to hard work, with the fiber of a
Paulista. With the young men Alfredo and Pradinho,
Ermengarda's behavior was different. She corrupted
her godsons by offering them the gold cigarette case
and cuff links that she herself had given me on my
birthdays. Not content with that, she took both of
them to bed at once, further endangering the stan-
dards of these young representatives of our finest
moral reserve. But the woman didn't stop at that. She
went on to Robert, the American spy, and from him
to the consul of Paraguay and even the consul of
Haiti. I struggled to unravel the system of abbreviations, which made the reading extremely difficult, for
I wanted to establish an exhaustive list so that even
the shadow of the slightest doubt could not be cast
upon the situation, but I couldn't because, unlike her,
I wasn't part of the swimming pool milieu. I knew
only the real names of some of the habitués and was
baffled by the abbreviations of the rest. I resolved
to study the matter scientifically and I would have
achieved some results on the day I began my methodical analysis, had I not been interrupted by Ermengarda's relatives from São Paulo. They defied the butler
and forced their way into my house to confer with me
about the thirtieth-day mass. I received them politely
but coldly, explaining that I was extremely busy and
had no time for masses or anything else. I begged
their pardon, but I could give them only five minutes.
I took advantage of the occasion to advise them: if
they really wished to organize the mass, at least they
should not send a notice to the papers, because of the
old people. They replied that everyone already knew
and would wish to attend the solemn event. I was ad-
amant that the mass should not be publicly announced. Not managing to change their minds, I gave

them two more pieces of advice: the newspapers were very meticulous on questions of orthography, it was no good writing Ermengarda with an *H* because the people at the copy desk would cross it off. Moreover, the seriousness of family matters under the heading "Obituaries" was well known. Under Brazilian law Ermengarda had no right to use my surname, even though she was dead. If she had died in Paraguay it might be different, but she had died here. They could send the death notice if they insisted, but with her maiden name or the name of her first husband, it didn't matter to me. The importunate visitors took their leave with their eyes popping out of their heads, and I was able to get back to my studies.

My job with the abbreviations was an arduous one. I established two rules and outlined others, but when the moment came to apply them to the blue notebook, science once again let me down. Such laws and rules are multifarious and tend to proliferate, each one dragging along its entourage of exceptions. I will limit myself to one example, the classic case of Paf. This abbreviation appears relatively often in the blue notebook. In accordance with my first general rule, it could be Pafúncio, the cat I always detested to the point of never even learning what it was called. But I couldn't overlook the principal exception to my second general rule, i.e., the license to use only the initials as an abbreviation, very common in the case of people with three names. (The diplomat Ilmar Pena Marinho, who was then beginning his brilliant career, was always Ipm for Ermengarda.) Given this order of things, Paf could perfectly well be Padre Antônio Faria, her confessor. I searched through the blue notebook for some decisive phrase—"Paf meowed" or "Paf prayed," but it was hopeless. The ambiguity created by the abbreviations prevailed; in the numerous situations described, the title bearer could have been either the cat or the priest, without the slightest incongruity. The frustration created for me by science, however, had the advantage of spurring me on to pure interior reflection, which I consider the ultimate method of knowledge. This time I came to believe that it was the only valid method, since it gave me such help in my understanding of Ermengarda. My point of departure was the Paf phenomenon, which I linked to one of the primary truths within anyone's grasp, in this case, Nature and the function of proper names. It is incontestable that the reality and credibility of the world—and therefore its equilibrium—rests largely in peoples' names. Upon waking each morning, we all confusedly feel the need to confirm that today's world is the same as yesterday's. This comfort can be found in the newspapers, through the names of people who continue to say, do, and write the very same things. The need for this reassurance is so urgent that it leads to exaggerated illusions. Our collective impression is that the dead under the heading ''Obituaries'' are always the same, unless at that moment we have some friend or relation who is very sick. When we go out, doormen, newspaper boys, and colleagues at work call us by our names, and they haven't changed theirs. Nor have the names of third parties to whom one necessarily alludes in everyday conversation altered. Now it was this harmonious mechanism, indispensable to mental health, that Ermengarda had tried to dismantle by her own invention or maybe even in cahoots with some subversive diabolical plot. Personally, I know of no stronger undermining force than that produced by her abbreviations. I experienced it in the flesh, with my own eyes and ears, first around the swimming pool and now with her diary. I saw chaos created; I saw it emerge from the blue notebook, whole and indivisible, to impose its universal will in Hermengarda's name—Hermengarda with an *H*, as she had decreed. Henceforward, her unhindered havoc,

I had come to this point in my reflections when I remembered that Ermengarda, in promulgating the Basic Law of Abbreviations to which all the general rules must submit, only did not invent an exception on her own behalf. She also had made exception in the blue notebook for my name, spread out various times on each page, written carefully to assure each of the eight horrible letters the most perfect visibility. Nevertheless, one had only to think briefly to see that we weren't dealing with an exception but with a particularly perverse formula for executing the Law against me. My case, the case of my given name, is unique. It was precisely by respecting it, saying it, writing it, that one arrived at the complete annihilation of my personality. This was the dominating impression left by my first reading of the blue notebook: Ermengarda wanted to destroy me. To do so she didn't limit herself to the brutal bombardment with *Polydoros* or the terrible nerve-attrition weapon of shortening names. She was an incomparably more subtle and ruthless warrior, capable of recourses never before glimpsed by military ingenuity. In the campaign of the blue notebook, her principal weapon was impatience. We all know that nothing more terrible exists. No situation in life is tolerable when we feel ourselves the object of other peoples' impatience. In childhood, the impatience of our parents or our teachers at school. Later, that of sweethearts, wives, and lovers; of our subordinates and superiors; of the person who listens or speaks to us, be it analyst or shoeshine boy. The impatience of our friends and enemies, of the priest who confesses and absolves us during our lives and gives us extreme unction. The impatience of the gravedigger, of our heirs and, most unbearable of all, God's impatience as we try to explain our lives to Him.

In the blue notebook I am oppressed by Ermengarda's impatience from beginning to end. She pardons me nothing, absolutely nothing. She browbeats me for pages on end because I didn't notice the purple notebook that she invariably carried with her: she would make a point of being where I would see her, pretend to write, act embarrassed, close the notebook as fast as possible to call my attention, but my slowness was surpassing, she wrote. My slowness was an absolute record: I would win in a contest of turtles or of turds. Her impatience increased as the pages turned; so did the number of times she wrote my name and other impolite things grew too. When I at last notice the purple notebook, Ermengarda showers me with sarcasm in the blue one, because I referred to an account book. She accuses me of not looking at the tablet open under my nose while she prolonged a fictitious telephone conversation, which is a flagrant injustice. Starting from the dinner with Dr. Cincinato, the dramatic tension heightens unbearably. The blue tablet doesn't know how to get P to read the purple notebook. The description of Hermengarda's suffering is so authentic that it makes one forget the sloppiness with which she writes. Really, Po's behavior is incomprehensible and even irritating. She strategically leaves the notebook open, pretending to be mysterious in order to arouse his curiosity, but Pol ambles by, absorbed in his thoughts and sees nothing. In these passages, as in so many others, the blue notebook says the strict truth and is right in being revolted at the absentmindedness of Poly but Polyd continues to wander about like a blind man in the middle of all these important events, forcing Hermengarda to travel to Jundiaí after dreaming up a foolproof plan—a silly story about car keys—to oblige Polydo to come face to face with the purple notebook, which took up half her dresser. To give Polydor even more of a chance Hermengarda decides to stay another night at Jundiaí and go to Campinas from there. She comes back and what does she find? The blue notebook can contain itself no longer and her fury explodes in every line. What does Hermengarda see? The purple notebook in the same place she left it, untouched, the dusting of face powder on its cover. Only a cuckold like Polydoro . . . but now he would see! And the blue notebook becomes threatening: Hermengarda would take that damned diary which had given her so much trouble, which had made her spend months and years bent over writing once, twice, three times, ten times, twenty times the same thing, to copy afterward into this miserable purple notebook—now she would take it and write in it with great big letters so that Polydor, who apparently was nearsighted besides being a cuckold, would find it on top of Hermengarda's unconscious body. She would write that she had killed herself because she had no more hope, but she hoped that Polydoro no (Polydoro no because Polydoro didn't like Polydoro) that Poly would pardon her and would find happiness with someone who loved him like poor Hermengarda had. The best thing would be to take a good dose of

sleeping pills. She was healthy as an ox, the doctor
had said, smiling. A few years ago, when she had suffered from insomnia, there was a night when she was
so desperate that she actually took ten—four first and
six more right afterward. But even so she had only felt
dizzy, had vomited afterward but didn't even need to
call the servant, yes, servant because her husband
didn't care, he would let his wife die and even be
pleased if she did. Now Hermengarda couldn't even
remember what insomnia was, at least the idiot dentist was good for that much. Now that she could
sleep, her health was better than ever. An ox. But she
didn't want to abuse herself, she would take only ten
and write the message. She would cry out, somebody
would come, they would call a doctor, and before
long her husband would arrive. Polydoro could be
reading the purple notebook while the doctor
pumped her stomach. If he didn't look at the notebook right away, then when she was pretending to
come to, she would tell him in a whisper that she had
nothing more to hide, he could read it all, everything,
without skipping a single line, and for him to forgive
her. This time she would go for broke. The last words
of the blue notebook ended in the middle of one of the
blank pages. There were only a few sheets left, and I
examined them to see if there might be some other
small notation. There wasn't, and all that whiteness
begged for more words, for the continuation of the
passionate, messy story. I smoothed my hand slowly
over the sheet, over the blue cover, I hugged the notebook hard, I wanted so much to help it, to help Hermengarda, but I couldn't, I didn't know how. In my
impotence I questioned Hermengarda: why had she
written that blue notebook? For me to read? Fatigue
made me confuse everything. That notebook hadn't

been prepared for me; Hermengarda hadn't had the intention of making me suffer when she wrote it.

I read the blue notebook over and over until I knew it almost as well as the purple one. It became a part of me in the tranquil life I led at home, postponing the day I would return to the agency. My partner was back again. My brothers, solicitous and silent, had brought him on one of their visits and we made peace almost without words. If any papers needed to be signed the secretary would bring them in the morning at breakfast time. On the first of these occasions she brought the copy of the ''Eulogy'' that I had complained about in another time, but I could see nothing wrong with her keeping it for herself. My large house had been transformed into a monastery with only one monk, attended by shadows as silent as myself. I thought about getting myself a cat to keep me company, for Pafúncio had run away only hours before the funeral. Probably he was afraid of facing my animosity alone. I put the idea of a cat aside. I am able to say I was happy.

During my study of the blue notebook certain points did not become entirely clear, and I felt the need to do some outside research. The events in Campinas during the Revolution of 1932 and the incident with the Paulista Association for Feminine Action intrigued me particularly. The blue notebook maintained that it had all been invented by Hermengarda to undo the impression she had given me with her scorn for the ''Eulogy to the São Paulo Lady.'' I had no doubt about the intention; I questioned the invention. I had a philosophic, calm admiration for Hermengarda that was unsurpassed by anybody else's, but that story wasn't typical of her powerful imagination. Its more characteristic products, like the abbreviations, had a degree of gratuity that was missing from the Campinas episode and its sequel featuring the PAFA. My academic side sensed in this tale a truth that could not have been improvised. Also, something caught my attention in the long biography of the new Procurator of the Republic published in the papers. In it I thought I recognized the onetime law student, the courteous young man who had received Hermengarda at the PAFA office. I considered visiting the association myself, or of running over to Jundiaí and Campinas where, talking with the old people and consulting newspapers of that period, I would doubtless gather data. But disappointment over my unproductive research in the abbreviational field deterred me, and this time I resisted the scientific siren song. The truth, not only about Campinas, the PAFA, or Hermengarda but about everything, could only come from within me. It would be the all-encompassing truth that would leave nothing unanswered. As usual I was in no hurry whatsoever. Let the truth reveal itself when the hour sounded; I would do nothing to precipitate it. In fact, it broke through from the innermost depths of my being but not solemn and contrite in the conventional form imagined by my pedantry.

I installed myself with habitual comfort in my new personality: a carefree rich man who had suffered a great displeasure and who lived quietly, passing his days in serene reverie, possessed of a vague intention of writing something about his feelings. I had devoured Hermengarda and her notebooks and was taking pleasure in the warmth of a prolonged digestion furnished me by material and moral wealth. The pink, purple, and blue Hermengardas were becoming more and more abstract, the mind's amenable tricks pushing all three toward oblivion. Occasionally I thought of her, but I thought mostly of myself. "Thought" is saying too much; I merely watched myself pass tirelessly through different moments of life, the scenes random and commonplace. Me in the Praça da República, watching the pigeons as I loitered about. Me attending the unveiling of a bust at the Commercial Association. Me greeting the mayor at the inauguration of a workers' village and so on. It was like the Brazilian newsreel clips, except the announcer's voice was substituted by my daydream monologue. The length of the subjects varied. I saw myself coming down Consolação Street before it was widened, deciding exactly as I came to the entrance of Xavier de Toledo beside the big wall and the tree, never again to forget that fortuitous instant completely devoid of meaning. Or coming out of the office, taking the car, and driving happily toward Altos dos Pinheiros, a tranquil neighborhood of provincial charm. As I drove I would be thinking about simple and varied things, the grape seller haggling with a housewife (naturally she wanted to choose the prettiest bunches), the vegetable man with the Italian accent, my bed and how good the pillow felt in the restful nights. I would arrive in front of my house set well back from the sidewalk, the trees of its spacious garden filtering and muffling the noise of the street as it reached the terrace. In contrast, the vulgar music of the cook's transistor radio blares from within. The butler must do something about this; I have already spoken to him. As in films, my mental images are not continuous. One scene cuts to another as though they have been spliced in the editing rooms of memory. Even now as I view my beloved real estate agency on a busy day, another image appears: the door of some ordinary room. Curious to see what is behind it, I cheat my reverie a little and force my imagination to look inside that room. It isn't just any room, but a bedroom. And in it I see Hermengarda, dead.

The film was suddenly interrupted. There was something strange behind me, inside me, as if a long, very thin stiletto—thinner than a thread and able to go straight through a person without drawing a drop of blood—had pierced me slowly at the back of my neck and was twisting inside me as it searched for my heart. The unbearably sharp sensation was closely followed by a wave of nausea that made me career through the hallways looking for a toilet where I could vomit. I have always feared diseases and know the symptoms of the principal ones. I searched anxiously for the name of this kind of attack, but in vain. The terms hemorrhage, thrombosis, stroke, and others jumbled themselves together. It was useless to fix on one of them, because I didn't have the pains characteristic of any. The effort of identifying a particular sort of pain revealed that I didn't have one. Without the support of words, which I grasped for at random, I would have lost my mind. I was saved by laying hold of the word *suffering*. It was suffering, I felt, without pain and without illness. The reassuring discovery allayed my panic and gave rise to a soft weeping that guided me carefully, avoiding errors and slipups, toward its motive: Hermengarda was dead.

The tranquil crying went on as long as it wanted to, without sobs, without sound and with very few tears. For days I was served at the table morning, noon, and night, and only hid the trembling of my lips behind the napkin or concealed my eyes with my hand when a servant approached. I slept and woke crying; there was no intermission.

When my tears dried up and I managed to look outside myself, there was not one stone left upon another in my house, in the neighborhood, in São Paulo, in the world.

The universe had turned to dust.

Her Times Two

First *Carnet*

I open this *carnet* to write of Her. The years I spend with Her are the calmest in a life fraught with hardships that I shall not here recall. If now, as I enter old age, my hour should come to long for repose, and I didn't have Her, the ideal to which my imagination should aspire would be a marriage exactly like ours. I rejoice at not having given ear to the insinuations and even warnings against my choice of Her as a wife. My close relatives and a colleague in my firm never ceased to allude to the numerous inconveniences in marriages where there is a great difference in age between the husband and the wife. I recognize that when I met Her—she must have been about sixteen—an abyss of time was evidenced by the difference in our physical appearances. Spiritually, however, we were always close. As the years passed, the disparity between Her and me lessened and when she became my wife at thirty, I had to make an effort to remember that she could have been my granddaughter. It was as if I had stopped in time and she had hastened to catch up. With her youth smothered beneath austere clothes, her appearance of early maturity was aided by that subtle yellowing of the complexion symptomatic of prolonged virginity. These two points, one subjective and one objective, i.e., my feeling of being young and Her virginity, complicated our wedding night, which was long and laborious. When it ended, its objective had not been achieved. I went so far as to blame this failure on my fallacious sense of youth, which hadn't taken the precaution of conferring with reality repeatedly and at short intervals. Yet the rigidity, not only of my character but of my whole spiritual and physical person, denied the truth of this idea. It was she who interrupted the awkwardness that moved into bed with us as we tried a succession of different positions. Discomfort had infiltrated my consciousness. She took charge and began to speak. First, she explained *us,* then she explained *me,* and finally she explained *herself,* using clarity and tact throughout. Her competence in the area of theory was extensive, as she had studiously followed various premarital courses ranging from those given by the Consolação parish church to the ones offered as an optional credit by the university entrance schools. Her reason for taking so many courses, when young girls generally studied only one, was explained by the length of time she took to marry—more than ten years. Now, during this time the nuptial science and its teaching, like other sciences (notably criticism and linguistics) underwent profound changes. She considered it her duty as a future wife to renew and enlarge annually her sum of knowledge in this field, and she was proven right on this first night which, without her accumulated instruction, could have caused me a long-lasting trauma, perhaps marked me for the rest of my life. I've already mentioned that after our various tries—the anniversary of which we celebrate every year with a bottle of champagne—she gave three short lectures: one about us, another about me, and a third about herself. The first centered on the concept of *gauge*, not in the offhand sense in which it is employed nowadays, but in the original technical meaning of calculation of proportions, standard measurement to which certain things ought to conform, like the distance between railroad tracks or the width of a tunnel, and the instruments used to verify such measurements. The initial explanation served as an introduction to the other two. In that which concerned me directly, her main theme was gauge, or caliber, which despite her premarital courses she had never imagined so well developed. This part of her dissertation, besides being very enlightening, had the benefit of soothing my self-esteem, which was somewhat battered at the moment. However, the best words she employed that night were used to describe herself. In addition to enriching my knowledge they touched me by revealing that it wasn't only her complexion that had altered during her long wait. To understand her discreet way of broaching this delicate aspect of the feminine condition, an elucidative parenthesis is necessary. Besides the premarital courses, she had taken numerous others, some of a professional order, such as typing, stenography, and English; others of a domestic nature (cooking, sewing, flower arrangement) and still others of miscellaneous types, such as one on binding and gilding books. This partial enumeration demonstrates her superiority over the young girls I knew who while waiting for husbands were wasting precious time on psychology, belles-lettres, or, most useless of all, pedagogy. Speaking of herself on that unforgettable night, she chose terms of comparison in the interesting area of bookbinding. As everyone knows (but I didn't), the celebrated and beautiful French *reliures* in wild boar

hide, made during the eighteenth century approximately up to the Revolution (with the decline of the
aristocracy pigskin was substituted for wild boar
hide) enter into a process of drying and wrinkling
which makes impossible not only the reading of the
volume but even its simple handling by admirers. It is
as if these books enter a profound withdrawal, saving
up riches which they can't use due to the impossibil-
ity of reading themselves, and at the same time deny-
ing curious potential readers the secret joys they
could bestow. One must not think, however, that she
had any special liking for metaphors. She used them
to safeguard her verbal modesty in speaking about
the humiliating phenomenon she had suffered. Right
afterward she went on to enumerate directly the mea-
sures to be taken: make an appointment with a gyne-
cologist for an incision with an electric bistoury, two
days to heal and all would be fine. There would be no
need for hospitals or stretchers; she would walk into
the specialist's office and out again.

She had been speaking continuously for almost half
an hour when I intervened to say that the next day we
would hunt up a doctor, but her quick mind already
had the name of her family physician, a Dr. Bulhões.
We went to his office in Marconi Street. *We* is only a
form of speech, because when we got to the door of
the building I backed out. I explained to Her that doctors' offices made me nervous—which was true—but
also I was embarrassed to meet this Dr. Bulhões, or
rather, to have him meet me. I would be waiting for
Her in a nearby tearoom situated at the rear of a bookshop. I waited for three hours. For the first hour, I remained seated at a table where I partook of hot
chocolate and cakes, but I felt uncomfortable occu-
pying a place for so long, in spite of the paucity of cus-

tomers. Only the bookshop section of the place was animated, where a group of young people were talking and laughing loudly. I ordered more chocolate and cakes and bore up for another hour. The rest of the time I spent pretending to look at books, but really I was extremely restless, first because she was taking so long—I feared some contretemps, one of those unforeseen events that are the rule in medicine once you go beyond routine stomach-thumping and chest-listening. The other, more immediate and disagreeable reason for my restlessness was the behavior of the group of people in the shop. Nobody noticed me during the first five minutes I spent in front of the shelves. They laughed a lot, jeering at one another and especially at certain respectable literary and political names. Upon noticing my presence, they began to talk more softly, as if I were bothering them. Then they whispered, obviously making comments about me. I decided to wait for Her on the sidewalk and look at the window display. But from inside they still watched me through the glass. A big robust boy got up with an air of decision and asked me if I wanted anything. He was not a clerk, and I replied firmly that I had had some hot chocolate and was waiting for my wife. The young man answered sarcastically that if she had delayed this long, she probably wouldn't come at all. I was about to raise my voice at his insolence when she appeared. I pointed to Her with triumph. Thinking the boy was somebody I knew, she extended her hand to him and the fellow, it must be said, behaved correctly, saying politely that the pleasure was his. My good humor restored, I said we must be going and we exchanged cordial farewells. Inside, the others watched the scene with interest, but there was no time for further introductions. I later learned that the bookshop crowd was made up of the new generation of São Paulo intellectuals, which struck me as odd, since they certainly didn't seem to take literature seriously. From what I could observe, they were extremists and perhaps had taken me for a defender of the social and political order, which in truth I am, but only in the area of ideas, not in the active function of a spy. Later I chanced to meet the owner of the establishment, a very refined gentleman who confided in me his dislike for that gang: they didn't buy books or drink tea and they spent the late afternoon—the best time of day for the serious clientele—raising a rumpus and frightening off customers.

As we walked to the car, our worries dissolved completely. Everything had gone very well. She had been delayed simply because Dr. Bulhões was terribly busy. The check I sent the next day was generous, but he deserved even more, for his competence had made a healing period unnecessary. That very night our marriage was consummated in the greatest comfort and we made up the time lost in the laborious vigil of the night before.

She had a way of facilitating everything. At the firm, where she had worked for so many years, she called me only doctor, the form of address for all men of position. I never explained my vague bachelor's degree to anyone in the circles I frequented, since I consider it unnecessary to justify being called doctor by defending a thesis. I was always called doctor at home by the servants and at work by my employees; doctor because I was the boss, a fact with which everyone agreed, including Her. When we became engaged she didn't change this form of address and in spite of using the familiar *you*, she continued to call me doctor. On our first wedding night she came out with an affectionate "my little doctor," which I didn't appreciate. On our real wedding night, she substituted that for "my big doctor," which was more adequate. The fact of people calling me simply doctor solved a delicate problem: my surname doesn't combine well with that form of address and my first name, though it doesn't combine with anything, is even worse when isolated. A horrible name I've been trying to keep hidden ever since the first humiliations in the kindergarten of the Escola Caetano de Campos; a name I try to forget. On our third night of marriage, she at last gave me an appellation which stuck. It sounded approximately like *pauldior,* pronounced very much à la française. Spoken softly during our caresses, it sounded like one of those erotic verbal compliments she had learned in her courses, the spontaneity of which is well known to specialists. The next morning, however, over coffee and newspapers, she continued to emit the same suggestive nocturnal syllables. I imagined she was making matinal overtures which would cause me to be late for work, but the absence of any provocative tone, as well as her satiated appearance, gave my thoughts a new direction. She was naturally alluding in a flattering way to the events of the night before and I began to answer the pauldiors with expressions like "my little woman" or "my darling," the only ones my creativity furnishes except when an authoritarian partner dictates what I should call her. Her sense of propriety was distressed at these words so unsuited to the moment, spoken within earshot of the malicious and ill-intentioned domestics who were hanging about, perhaps listening at the door. It was only then that I realized that for more than eight hours she had been

calling me by my name. Now, this name had traumatized my spirit to such a degree that I even avoided
words that had a similar sound, like *polyglot*
or *polyester*; I would actually grow apprehensive
when I heard records of the old brand Polydor. My idiosyncrasy reached into distant verbal areas as when,
still young, I showed my friends the envy I had of
flowers possessing multiple masculine organs; or
later, when I reached maturity, I criticized in the same
circles women who have more than one man at a
time. But I never used the word *polyandrous* (back
then written in Portuguese with a *y*), a current expression in the select circles I was part of. Nevertheless,
spoken by Her, my name was transformed so much
that this time the acceleration of my heart was caused
by pleasure, not by the old fear provoked when I was
four years old by the cruel children who used to pursue me screaming my name across playgrounds and
through corridors until I would hide in the latrine,
awaiting the bell that would free me from the fury of
the young jackals. In Her mouth, the sounds that had
made me suffer so much became a source of joy. In
truth, the sounds were others, since she spoke the
four syllables in a way unrecognizable to outsiders,
especially servants. The first two syllables almost
turned into Paul, a handsome name in any language
and sufficiently removed from the combination po-ly.
Her pronunciation altered still more the other two syllables, do-ro. Between the *d* and the *o* she insinuated a
caressing *i* that practically annulled the final *o*, in such
a way that one clearly heard *dior*. Moreover, as she
also separated the first two syllables from the last two,
I received a new name and surname as well: Paul
Dior, very flattering to the French side of my personality.

I could mention other examples of Her kindness in the face of my little peculiarities, which outsiders might consider weaknesses but which are part of my being, and without which I would be someone else and not the very reasonable man I am. She, at any rate, accepts me as I am, creating about me a climate of restfulness. She is attentive to all that concerns me and shares my small interests with enthusiasm. A few references to the periods we regularly spend in Águas de São Pedro will serve to illustrate. A tenacious case of arthritis obliges me to take periodic cures at the sulphuric springs. She always accompanies me, doing her best to find a motive in her own physical state so as to leave me completely at ease. She spends days taking doses calculated to the centimeter from the Almeida Salles, Giaconda, or Juventude fountains, and advertises to the maximum their effect on her complexion, sleep, and stomach so I won't think she puts up with such monotony exclusively for my sake. Her consideration for me has no limit. I mentioned the small interests that lend some variation to my present life, which turns completely upon the axles of home and office. As I no longer like to read or attend movies, theaters, or exhibitions, and as television puts me to sleep, I find diversion in the things I see in the street or in the places I go to have coffee. There isn't much variety: facades from the twenties, cement lions, and the scenes painted on blue tiles in the bars of our capital city. I usually am alone when I admire these sights, walking to or from work in spite of having two cars. Walking is good for me. In Águas de São Pedro the two of us walk together a lot, and to pass the time we enter all the places we pass: hotels, bazaars, restaurants, gas stations, branch offices of state and federal savings banks, and cafés. In one of the latter, called Delight's Bakery and Bar, I discovered a picture that aroused my continued interest: medium-sized, it represented a little girl holding a turkey. I wanted to go back to Delight's on the pretext of drinking a cup of the awful coffee they serve, buying a pack of cigarettes I don't smoke, or asking for a useless box of matches, just to contemplate that child with her bird. At first I didn't do so because of Her, fearing to bore her, but it was she who took the initiative. One afternoon we were vaguely looking into one of the savings banks when she pondered that there wasn't much to see there and suggested we go back to the bar with the girl and the turkey. From then on she acquired the habit of talking to the regular customers of the bar, old people of the region who knew many things. They would explain the difference between the andorinha bird, which had practically disappeared from Águas de São Pedro, and the andorões which to this day crowd the TV antennas as the afternoon wanes. They would recall stories about the early times of the region, when the pioneers were drilling for oil and discovered the waters that cure rheumatism. Not realizing this, they left the gigantic spring gushing for years. Everyone was friendly toward Her, and as they talked I would stare at the girl and her turkey, participating absently in their conversation.

There is still so much I could say. The pleasure I find in writing about Her here in Águas or in the office in São Paulo, during the empty hours of the early afternoon! At times it's hard for me to remember her real name, I've become so accustomed to calling her Her, that is, ever since she came to work for the firm so many years ago. Many times I made her repeat the story of this nickname—a little story I never tire of hearing. They had a slightly feebleminded cook who agreed to work for her modest family (father, mother, and a younger brother) in exchange for room and board and some occasional cast-off clothes. This simple soul, a fine person and a good cook, was incapable of remembering names and called the father Mr., the mother Mrs., the younger brother Him, and her Her. The family found this amusing and adopted the curious system of names, calling each other Mr., Mrs., Him, and Her. When the old woman went to the poorhouse, everyone in the family reverted to their real names except Her. At school, when they asked her name, she answered spontaneously that it was Her and the director approved, recalling the title of a celebrated English novel and its heroine. Her name became Her permanently. From this story emanated a rather sad poem that I always associate with a small cement lion stationed on the pillar of a gate in Maria Antônia Street. And with the girl holding the turkey. Actually, one of Her charms is her indefinable melancholy. The first time I sensed it was when she broached the subject of her virginity at the beginning of our romance.

She had already been an employee of the company for several years, and our working relationship was excellent. Eventually we came to speak of more personal subjects, though the distance between employer and secretary was not diminished. My private life was not as easy as it is today; I had many worries, and to all effects was married, since I had no reason to go noising abroad the fact that legally my marriage didn't exist. Once I asked Her to type the first draft of a contract where my complete name and civil status had to appear. I myself would normally type this kind of document, the introduction to which the other party never reads, making improbable the embarrassment of their seeing my first name, but on that day I lost track of things and ended up giving Her the rough draft along with some other papers. When she came in holding my original and saying I had made a mistake, my heart sank; I was certain she had seen my name. But no. She only discovered the latter when she insisted on reading our marriage contract, and I've already noted the admirable way she found of circumventing the problem three days after we were married. What she had thought was a mistake was the designation of my civil status as "single." I explained in a summary manner, without going into detail, that under Brazilian law I actually was single. At that very instant I sensed that there stirred in Her a new interest toward me, which was borne out only later. She never spoke to me about it, but it's possible that even then she perceived my domestic difficulties and felt sorry for me, making a special effort to be an efficient worker, with a maternal warmth that did me good. At that time I thought of myself as incredibly older, and I was amused at being cared for like a child. So young, I thought, but like all women she's a potential mother seeking at least a psychic realization in selfless affection. I confess that during all those years I never saw anything in Her beyond the attentive helper who doubled as the vigilant little mother of an almost-old man, capable of serving him with unchanging dedication, pledged to providing quietly all the dozens of small things indispensable to his wellbeing. As I think back, I discover that one of Her greatest moments was shown in her easy delicacy when she came to me in that crucial period mature men pass through: the interval, as difficult as some phases of adolescence, between consummate maturity and senility that fails to arrive. Her historic mission in my biography was to give new dimension and vitality to this chapter, transforming a time which would have been merely transitional into something valuable in its own right, as if instead of old age, what I had been waiting for were Her. The fundamental lever in this miracle was Her virginity. When we first touched on this matter it was the number one mark of my new existence, the zero mark being the luminous morning when she confessed she loved me. This event occurred two or three years after the conclusion of my first marital crisis. Her declaration did me a world of good, although only of a spiritual nature; the distrustful body did not accompany the spirit. When one cold evening I took her to a nightclub, then rare in São Paulo, the comfort I sought at her side had no intimation of pleasures more concrete than a good dinner and a high-quality wine. The direction our encounter took was not planned, and I was the first person to be surprised when I kissed her and delicately proposed we become lovers. The moment she replied in her tiny voice that she was a virgin was the sharpest of my entire life. Mutation, metamorphosis, crystallization, rebirth, horizon, discovery, phoenix, lustrum, resolution, decision, revolution; I would need to use all these words with mastery to describe what I felt. Still, I think I made my basic feeling clear as it came from the depths of the collective masculine memory of the species. I should explain that none of the women who had crossed or accompanied my path up to then had ever been a virgin. In spite of my conservative upbringing, I never gave virginity excessive importance and tended, like the moderns, to consider it an outmoded taboo. All this on the theoretical plane. In practice, I was more severe, and even advised the younger members of my family to exercise prudence when the time came for them to choose wives, inclined as they were to discard with excessive haste a tradition that, like all traditions, has a certain reason for being and needs to be analyzed and understood. On the other hand, more than once I had started a home with experienced women. It's true that things never worked out, but I do not attribute that misfortune exclusively to the circumstance of these ladies' not being beginners. Her virginity brought a new freshness to my aging worldliness, and my imagination broke out of its seemingly permanent lethargy.

I come to the final pages of this *carnet* and there is still so much I could say. Perhaps I'll start another one, I don't know. But it is necessary to register here that Her love for me is greater and has much more merit than mine. Who would have thought that the autumn of my life would hold for me a woman of such quality and truth?

I write these final lines at home, an exceptional circumstance since I never bring the *carnet* here; I wouldn't forgive myself the absentmindedness of letting it fall into Her hands to offend her sense of modesty. At this exact moment I've been writing for more than half an hour in the bathroom. I hear Her voice, affectionate and slightly worried: "Paul Dior, you've been in there such a long time! Did something happen, Paul Dior? Answer, Paul Dior!"

My only worry, which I make an effort to keep at a distance, is the fragility of Her health, which obliges her constantly to visit doctors' offices, clinics, and health centers. Fortunately she doesn't need to be hospitalized, for if that ever happened I don't know what I'd do; my idiosyncrasy toward everything concerning medicine has grown alarmingly pronounced with my age. Before, it was enough for me to stay away from places where medical science was practiced; I even avoided simple contact with doctors. Judging by the number of new hospitals and clinics being built everywhere in the city, the health of our population is deteriorating frightfully, and I don't see the public authorities taking any notice of this grave problem. Sooner or later even the neighborhood where I live will be sacrificed. I already had to bribe a functionary of the Public Health Service who wanted to start a childrens' clinic right here in Alto dos Pinheiros; from the look of it, children haven't escaped the general decline in health either. I know I won't be able to resist for very long. When my neighborhood is invaded, I'll move to Águas de São Pedro where there are no hospitals and the one doctor limits himself to prescribing the dosage of waters and the temperature of the baths. I can shake his hand without being attacked by the itching that comes over me at the mere sight of the Clinical Hospital when I forget myself and pass along Avenida Rebouças. Her way of protecting me—afflicted as she has always been by poor health, and consulting specialists almost daily—is the ultimate example of her dedication and must be recorded. The distribution of Her time is organized in such a way that I never know which is the day she doesn't go to the doctor; I always have the impression that it is precisely the present day. Yesterday has already gone by and tomorrow doesn't yet exist, and since (thank God) my happiness is neither retroactive nor anticipatory, memory and imagination do not provoke my itching. What I must avoid are the visual or olfactory evidences, and she manages so that these never come near me. Upon coming home, I find Her bathed and perfumed, without the slightest vestige of injections marring that skin I know so well or the small blue veins whose pulsation I press with such affection. I imagine she must substitute intramuscular or intravenous shots with medications that can be administered in other ways, but the boxes and bottles of medicine that might exist in our house are certainly better concealed than the safe where I keep my stock certificates from Light, Paulista Railways, etc. I also have shares in Melhoramentos and other lesser-known but equally valuable companies. In short, in spite of knowing she is sickly I never perceive it and live in peace. The moments, like this one, when I think about the subject are so rare that I can affirm I am completely happy. Although Her precarious health is at this moment the only cloud in my sky, I don't believe that Destiny would commit the insensitivity of taking Her away from me. Other women besides Her have attributed this constant optimism of mine to egotism, but they were less understanding.

Second *Carnet*

Fresh facts, deserving to be recorded, demand that I open a new *carnet* about Her without which the first, which I wrote a few years ago, would become incomprehensible to me. The tranquillity of Águas de São Pedro, where I have come for relief from a particularly sharp attack of arthritis, brings me face to face with the unpleasant duty of filling this second notebook. I have chosen one with a larger number of pages; I have more to write in this one than in the other, and I respect the superstition that pages left blank in a used notebook are a bad omen and presage the cutting off of life. In spite of everything, I don't wish Her any ill, nor myself either, but the fact is, everything has changed. I am not able to say just when the alteration began and I don't know its causes. The reasons she presented in the recent argument that precipitated our separation seem unclear to me. I will not describe in detail the gradual poisoning of our relationship; the process took years, during which the dust of ill feeling kept on accumulating and in the end became unbearably suffocating. If it weren't for the terrible verbal explosion of a week ago—an explosion which had a salutary effect on me—I think I would have pined away and died of the special type of tedium caused by mediocre unhappiness.

I had arrived home lighthearted, prepared for the tiredness that punctually overcame me. I found Her with a new gleam in her eye, herald of decisions. I waited. During dinner she didn't say a single word. She waited for the servants to retire; happily (or un-happily) up to the end of our relationship she was dis-creet around third parties. Once we were seated in the small lounge where we had our coffee, she began. I heard Her out with polite attention and resolved not to interrupt her, a system I had adopted during the last two years, with reasonable success. She usually would talk calmly for about an hour, using impecca-ble language. The content of what she said, always the same, consisted of a list of general complaints about the life she led and criticisms of my fastidious, egotistical, comfort-loving, and false behavior. This behavior was demonstrated particularly, according to Her, in the silence I adopted during these rituals.

117

They only tired me physically, a problem I couldn't get around since, always constrained by good manners, I would never leave a lady to talk to herself, especially in this case, as the insults and laments were couched in polished, civilized words. During those dozens of months she never accused me of anything specific with names and dates, nor did she suggest a solution. She was waiting for me to do so, and I'd had many ideas on how to free myself from that ritual which threatened to go on indefinitely. She and I were like two businessmen who want to make a deal but keep stalling for time, each hoping that the other will make the first proposal. On that night she began as usual, but I was alerted by a new word. The usual expressions answered their roll call: *fastidious, wearisome, vexatious, annoying*—and its variant *annoyance*—but when she said outright I was a *bore*, I perceived something different in the air, and my interior attention corresponded, for once, to the attentive face I always maintained. The continuation of her speech confirmed that the old ritual had undergone a transformation as great as those of the mass, or actually even greater, as was verified in the course of the evening. She alluded with new directness to my arthritis, to my cures in Águas where she had suffered the humiliation of being the wife of the most comic figure the porters had ever seen in the constantly changing population of the spa. Example? The entire village commented about my passion for that ridiculous little girl hugging the turkey. At this point she paused as though expecting a reaction. There was none. She resumed: actually I knew her very little, because in spite of being sly I wasn't intelligent; on the contrary I demonstrated a surpassing foolishness. She cited the fact of my never having wondered about that brother of hers whom I'd never met. He lived in Rio, but every time we traveled there, he was in the North or the South. In fact, on this point I showed not only foolishness but also lack of family spirit and hardness of heart, since during our life together I had never visited her parents' graves in the Quarta Parada cemetery, nor even those of my own parents, much closer, in Consolação. But the really extraordinary thing was my lack of curiosity to meet this brother. Just as well: this so-called brother didn't exist. No?! No. The Him of Her childhood with the simple cook was an orphaned cousin taken in by her parents. He was the same age as Her. Another, shorter pause creating the impression she had made a mistake. She started talking again, faster, apparently anxious to reach a point at which something was supposed to happen. Her and Him grew up together and until they were ten or eleven, slept in the same narrow bed in the little room which gave onto the plum tree in the back garden. Curious and complacent, they played at the childish game of discovering the differences between boys and girls with complete naturalness. The game was interrupted when they grew too big for one bed and slept in separate ones in the same room. Even after she got to be fifteen, when she slept alone in the room and he left to occupy the living room couch, the games continued. She closed this part of her explanation by saying that she and the cousin were the teachers and students in her first course in premarital education: first and only, she concluded. And waited. Her wait was in vain despite the lengthy pause. My silence was not a mere civility; I was prodigiously interested in the plot and anxious for it to continue. She began again, with a reference to a medical exam which I didn't quite understand, then drew back and passed quickly to another subject. With a resolute air, she said solemnly that in view of the circumstances, she imagined I would like a divorce. I had been waiting for this proposal for a long time, but the moment was inopportune; just then the only thing that interested me was the continuation of the story. This time there was really a very long silence. I was afraid that if I didn't say something she wouldn't open her mouth again for the rest of the night. She had taken the initiative of making a concrete suggestion and was awaiting my opinion. On any other occasion I would have answered affirmatively, depending on her intentions, of course. But if we started discussing this now, the conversation would take a practical turn and I would never know anything more about Him and Her, still only fifteen years old. I was obliged to improvise and in my panic I said the wrong word, which turned out to be providential. I meant to ask her if in our situation a separation was reasonable, but instead of "situation" I said "age." She replied vehemently that I shouldn't confuse our ages, she had given me the best years of her life but she was still a girl compared to an old wreck like me, the cousin was the one who was Her age. The appearance of the word "wreck" for the first time in our conversation, and the return to the cousin, seemed like good omens and induced me once again to be silent. Sure enough, after a few words of sarcasm, she took up her story at the point where she had left off. When they reached adolescence, the cousin became more imprudent and daring, but she knew how to put Him in his place, thus safeguarding her virginity. The new pause was prolonged, probably because she misinterpreted my impatience, the nature of which was similar to that produced by the television commercials that interrupt a soap opera or film, with the difference that Her story was incomparably more interesting than those on TV.

At this point she went back to the medical examination she had precipitately introduced in a foregoing passage. Its significance only now became clear. She had been slightly hurt, and her mother, who knew Her recently commenced but very regular menstrual dates by heart, was alarmed by the blood she found on the sheets. She obliged Her to undergo a medical examination. They knew a doctor from the Santa Casa, a worthy young man for whose family Her father had worked as a chauffeur. This same doctor had arranged a place in the poorhouse for the old cook. By this time, she had already mentioned the doctor's name several times, but I only understood this later. It took me awhile to recognize the name Bulhões from the way she pronounced it. She didn't include the *Dr.* and practically swallowed the first letter, so that I didn't catch the meaning of the ". . . ulhões" that began to appear with a certain frequency. The doctor examined her with utmost care, affirmed that she was intact as far as the principal matter was concerned, and as he tinged the secondary problem with iodine, asked why a smart, pretty girl like her would do a thing like that—because she enjoyed it or because it was a habit? She didn't quite understand the range of the question, and limited herself to answering simply that she didn't much enjoy it, but she didn't want to run the risk of never getting married. That day the doctor didn't say anything more. In the waiting room he reassured the mother as to Her virginity. There was nothing serious wrong with Her, just a small disturbance common in adolescence. In a short time she would be fine and needed only some shots that he himself would give her. He preferred that she be brought to his office in José Bonifácio Street (Marconi Street didn't exist then) because the Santa Casa was for beggars, and he insisted on taking good care of the daughter of an old servant of his family's. The next day, the doctor jokingly asked if she needed more iodine and then went on to explain many things, illustrated with charts and pictures in books. Next he proposed that she relax. He promised on his word of honor as a doctor: whenever she ordered, he would reconstitute her virginity. As she was naturally delicate, two small stitches would be sufficient, maybe only one, even taking into account the growth factor, for she wasn't yet sixteen.

During the next pause, which she threatened to prolong unduly, I discovered a way of making Her continue, which worked well to the end. The rest of the time I talked only when I wanted to. Each time she interrupted her narrative and waited for me to say something, my face would acquire an expression that seemed to ask, "and then?" which had the effect of making Her go on—rather irritably, it's true, which was inconvenient as the increasing pitch of her voice might reach the kitchen. However, soon it became unnecessary to goad her on. She seemed to be confessing her memories to herself while she addressed me. In this abandon the name ?ulhões reacquired a consonant that didn't correspond to the original *B*. The reason for this intrigued me until the narrative provided an explanation. When she remembered I was listening, she created an ambiguous sound that belonged simultaneously to the first two consonants of the alphabet. Indeed, up to the final seconds of that long evening, Her language remained correct and for the last time I was able to admire the mastery of

speech of that girl of such humble origin. It was evident that in place of the mythical premarital courses,
and in addition to the one on bookbinding, she had
taken many others, both public and private. These
must have included one on elocution (pioneered in
high society by Dona Noêmia Nascimento Gama) for
as I transcribe and condense Her words, I seem to be
hearing the sonority of her voice, worked up to the
point of artifice.

''. . . ulhões kept his promise. Of the many he
made, it was the only one he kept rigorously, without
batting his long eyelashes which have become golden
with time. You never met him; you didn't wish to, so
you have no way of imagining his eyelashes. In their
abundance they resemble those of the writer whose
photograph you showed me in the library beside the
Leopoldo Fróis Theater, the only difference being that
that man was ugly, and Bulhões was very handsome.
I recognize that he really couldn't keep some of his
promises. He failed to marry me only because his
wife's weak lungs were aided by the discoveries of
medicine. When she finally died, I had already gotten
tired of waiting and married you. The proof of his
good faith was his desire to separate from the mori-
bund wife, but I couldn't break the promise I made to
my mother on the night she died: to get married prop-
erly, with all the papers in order, notarized by the
civil authorities and the priest. I often renewed this
promise in front of the shallow grave where she was
buried beside my father; it remains shallow because
you never kept your promise to order the statue with
the two angels that I saw in the funeral home on
Alagoas Street. In this case, Bulhões showed greater
sensibility; he wanted to pay for the statue. I thought
it wouldn't be right in spite of our intimacy, as great

as that which you and I shared when we were happy. I don't want to be unfair to anyone. You were the two men in my life and when I was still happy, I think I was able to be equitable to both of you. At least I tried. I'll give you an example. Bulhões knew I called you Paul Dior and asked me to give him the same proof of affection, transforming his name as well. I asked him if he disliked his name too and he said he was bothered by the *B* and added, laughing, that he preferred the neighboring consonant. From then on, as with Paul Dior for you, I always called him by this name, behind closed doors of course, at a safe distance from the nurses and assistants in the places where he worked: his office, the Santa Casa, the Portuguese Beneficiary Home, the Matarazzo Health Center, and the Clinical Hospital, after it was inaugurated by Ademar de Barros. All served for our rendezvous. At first we met almost daily, then less frequently, and nowadays we rarely see each other and then only to talk. But I don't want to think about the present, equally bitter for me with you or with him; I want to remember the golden era with the two of you, when Culhões—better educated than you—said gorgeous things to me using words you never used. On my heart are engraved forever his remarks about how delicate my body was—which didn't impede, he would say, my being a master polyandrist and the happy territory of a diarchy. This isn't the time for insincerity; I loved Culhões much more than Paul Dior, but as long as I was happy I had enough dedication and patience for both. It's true that I would have preferred to marry him, and when you got old and arthritic, ever more set against doctors, I had the hypothesis that, if we were both widowed, I might finally marry him. He answered that he hadn't thought of this, but if he were to do so, he would choose a younger woman. I am certain you would never offend me so blatantly—one must give credit where it's due—but still we must pardon Culhões, who was going through a difficult phase. Always vain—I would even say pretentious—about himself, Culhões, like all of your sex, would blame his partner for the decline which fatally accompanies age; in men, naturally. And like all of your sex—*you* seem to be an exception—he nurtured an incurable nostalgia for his youth. I thought about Culhões when I read the latest interview with the old soccer star Garrincha, where he recalls with emotion his repeated goals during the great matches here and in foreign countries. Culhões was also very well traveled and, like the champion, had reason to be proud of his past. He was brilliant, not only in São Paulo and Rio, but also in London, Paris, and Berlin, from whence he brought me distinguished diplomas hanging on the waiting room wall. His obsessions didn't bother me as long as life was happy; I've already said that as long as I was content I had patience for you both. Searching my memory I can only remember one occasion when I got irritated with both of you at the same time, but it didn't last long. It was when we had just gotten married. I had asked Culhões to take only one stitch, but he insisted on taking an extra one as a security measure, or so he said. He could have been right; I didn't know you and couldn't have guessed, to inform him, up to what point you are absentminded about these things. Naturally he imagined, judging for himself, that you belonged to the nosy, investigating type who would want to know, see, and smell everything. You know as well as I do the results of your prudence—no, I'm not disputing how competent you are, I could test this and the results couldn't be more flattering to your skill. After he sewed me up, as a duty to my conscience, I resolved to undergo an examination at the Institute of Legal Medicine; my cousin has a part-time job there and made things easier. The certificate they furnished me could figure beside Culhões's foreign diplomas as additional proof of his knowledge. Even so, our wedding night was a nightmare for me. How I controlled my nerves to avoid the explosion of impatience that would have compromised everything! You have no idea how I strained my imagination to produce the long speech about gauge and caliber, for in reality, next to Culhões you were small fry. Don't think I remained unjustly impatient with you over this point for which the other was exclusively responsible. On our first morning as a married couple (in name at least) I thought about this, and being scrupulous I was remorseful for my feelings of the night before. I changed my mind by the end of the afternoon and if you're honest you will agree with me. While you waited for me in that bookshop you afterward detested for the rest of your life, I poured out to Culhões all the accumulated irritation of the night, blaming him for the impasse. He admitted that perhaps he had been wrong to take excessive precautions. After I described to him your preference for total darkness and the classic embrace, he was convinced that one stitch would have been quite enough, or who knows, none at all. I rejected this last suggestion with vehemence, since it seemed to violate a point implicit in the promise I had made to my deceased mother, but my friend demonstrated my reasoning as absurd and ended up making me agree to the proposal he made. He wasn't convinced that the blame was entirely his, and, after a few theoretical considerations about anatomy, was

anxious to put his thesis to a practical test. I still felt
that a bistoury incision would be preferable to elimi-
nate the superfluous stitch, but his renewed arguments had a recognizable validity. He reminded me
that the night before you had had a psychologically
intimidating experience, and that the slightest obstacle might assume for you the guise of an insurmountable barrier. Besides, one mustn't forget that you
were no longer young; the best thing for all three of
us would be a natural solution. We should at least try,
and only resort to medical intervention if his efforts
that afternoon should prove as useless as yours of the
night before. He repeated that it would benefit you
for the reasons he had explained, and me because it
would make the incision unnecessary. For himself,
the interest in trying would be above all professional:
he must find out if he had been wrong or not to take
the second stitch. Having no answer to give, I agreed.
In truth, Culhões triumphed, but if he had been less
pretentious he would have agreed with me that the
second stitch had definitely been an error. If you had
a lengthy wait in that bookshop it was because things
weren't resolved with the ease that Culhões in his
boastfulness imagined. He had a hard battle, strug-
gling continuously at first, then resting from time to
time to get his strength back. When he won, vain as
always, he had the bad taste to compare himself ad-
vantageously to you, forgetting his own argument of
an hour before concerning your age. I am convinced
that you too would have been capable if you weren't
so emotional, if you had had more self-confidence.
Your age was no problem and your instrument, incomparably narrower than Culhões's, was actually an
advantage in the circumstances. But this is past.
Everything went well and I'll never forget the years of

happiness I owe the two of you. I would hope you in turn might remember all I've done. I've already given up hope of the slightest acknowledgment from Bulhões; he's turning into a poor devil whose mania is staying young, surrounded by a growing group of young girls who fleece him of his money while, in the same proportion, the clients who furnish it diminish. He will come to a sad end. With you it's different; you're a tranquil old man who has known how to age gracefully. Thus we come to my situation. I still have a few years of youth left, and as I wish you a long life, I know that when you die I'll be an old woman, heiress to a useless fortune. The idea of becoming a sad though rich widow horrifies me. I want a separation. For you it makes no difference, but for me there's still time. I will know how to use whatever comes to me of our property. Today my cousin is the best bookbinder in the city; all he needs is some initial capital to enlarge his studio and dedicate himself exclusively to the trade. At present he is obliged to waste time at the Institute of Legal Medicine. Together we will be partners in a great firm, and I will be happy again; you know how I've always liked bookbinding.''

I saw that this pause was final; she had nothing more to add. I had followed her tale most attentively without letting my mind wander even once, as proven by the fidelity with which I reproduce the story a week later. I was strongly moved by a variety of feelings. It was the first time I had ever heard such a spontaneous confession, formulated moreover with a certain talent. This experience must be commonplace for priests, psychiatrists, and a few foreign police officials; I don't believe the Brazilian ones ever get that kind of confession. When they aren't dealing

128

with potential confessors—by definition distrustful—
they hear only lies. If they use other methods, the
truths they extract along with the fingernails of the in-
terlocutor are only scraps of truth belonging to a
beaten body and spirit. But to hear the confession of a
mouth and soul palpitating with ambiguity, although
it may be an everyday experience for the professional
confidants, was enough to alter the life of an amateur
like me. Not that mine was: I'm getting old and my
reactions are slow. But there was another motive for
my holding back. The one thing that upset me in Her
narrative—which I followed almost the whole time as
a story unconnected with me—was Her representa-
tion of Dr. Bulhões as a person better educated than
I, the word "educated" used in the sense of "cul-
tured." Very well, I am fairly modest intellectually
but I frequented intelligent circles and knew perfectly
well the meaning of the words "polyandrist" and
"diarchy" that Dr. Bulhões had taught her. The first I
never used for the private reasons described in the
first *carnet;* "diarchy" I never used for lack of opportunity. Besides Russia, an alarming country I discuss
as little as possible, no other government run by two
sovereigns exists. I wanted to make Her see that I
wasn't as ignorant as she thought, and I found the
opportunity by asking her about a detail which hadn't
been fully clarified. I told her that the word "polyandrist" that Dr. Bulhões had applied to her seemed
correct to me, as well as the derivative adjective
"polyandrous." There was no doubt she had had
more than one husband at the same time, since the
prolonged years of intimacy with Dr. Bulhões permit-
ted her inclusion in this category. Even if there had
been other men, the word *polyandrist* was not limit-
ing and would remain valid. About "diarchy" I had

doubts, and I asked her if in truth her body, in spite of its smallness, hadn't been the territory of a triarchy. She didn't understand because undoubtedly she never heard that word, so thus I got my revenge. Still, I remained curious and I repeated the question in a simpler, more direct form. I wanted to know if, during the time she lived with me, when she visited and was visited by Dr. Bulhões in high hospital beds, she had also been her cousin's lover. A smile crossed Her face before she replied. She began by explaining her amusement. Decidedly, men were all alike. For example, Dr. Bulhões and I, apparently so different, had reacted in an identical way to a given situation. Dr. Bulhões had never been jealous of me but had harassed her with questions about the cousin and I, upon learning the whole story, had accepted Culhões but resisted the idea of the other. I replied irritably, accentuating the B of Bulhões, that I hadn't accepted or refused the doctor or the cousin, I simply considered myself well informed about one and uninformed about the other. Gently she began speaking again and dissipated the bad humor brought on by the fuss. She confessed that really she never had heard the word "triarchy," but now that she knew what it meant, she didn't consider it accurate to define the relationship linking herself, Dr. Bulhões, her cousin, and me. As the entire argument was based on considering her body a territory, she thought it necessary to make clear that the area in which Dr. Bulhões and I exercized our double sovereignty wasn't the same as that where the first man exercized his: he remained faithful to the memories of adolescence. She asked if the use of the word "triarchy" would be accurate under these conditions. I agreed that it wouldn't, admiring once more Her capacity to learn.

There was one more question I wanted to ask but I thought it better to consider her testimony finished. I wanted to know if the three of us had been the only important men in Her life or if there were still others. I did right to contain my curiosity. The introduction of new characters would make the story at risk of becoming wearisome and, in the final analysis, less admirable. I decided the other things I wanted to say would be better said in a different situation. They were a few practical hints about the viability of a great bookbinding firm. The idea seemed utopian to me; furthermore, I didn't know anything about the cousin's real aptitude. I was afraid she might lose in this adventure the reasonable but after all modest sum I was disposed to give her—as long as she agreed to a definitive, irreversible contract of discharge to accompany our amicable, discreet, and (insofar as possible) secret separation. My family had snubbed us *en masse* ever since my engagement to Her, and I couldn't bear the idea of the remaining members thinking they had been right to criticize and warn against my marriage. I am a liberal conservative who respects other peoples' traditions, but I'm subversive when it comes to family; I can't stand mine. I'd be capable of handing over to Her half of what I have just to avoid their learning about the separation and being amused by it. And that half represented a fortune after the skyrocketing of the Petrobrás shares I had bought trembling with fear, since people were saying back then that it was a communist business. Newspaper rumors! But there was no reason to be worried about the separation with regard to my property. She would be content to leave me and take whatever my generosity offered her. She would live in a world of bookshops and libraries where no relative of mine would ever come near her and no one would know about anything. If by chance she should die before I did, which after the revelation of her stupendously good health seemed very unlikely to me, I was to make some arrangement with the cousin. I would take care of all the expenses, send the notice to the papers with her married name, bury her in the family plot in Consolação unless she had left instructions to be laid to rest with her family in the Quarta Parada. But above all, I would be present in the inevitable churches and cemeteries to receive, in the role of inconsolable widower, the condolences of whatever relatives were still alive, since it would be excessive to hope that they would all be dead. I saw nothing inconvenient in having the cousin at my side helping me receive sympathies since he was, after all, Her last carnal relative, that is, granted they really were cousins. The old cook in the poorhouse, if she ever existed, had already died and probably wouldn't be able to say whether or not they were related, since mental disability worsens with time. To get in touch with the old woman's institution, I would need to contact Dr. Bulhões. If he were still alive and practicing, I might avoid the clinic and my attacks of itching by making an appointment to meet him in the bookshop next door, if it were still there. It must have changed a great deal; the young intellectuals wouldn't even recognize me. They would have changed too, grown comfortable. Maybe they wouldn't even be there anymore, their time taken up by well-paid positions in the press, government administration, or private enterprise. I would never see them again, but even so the time had come when we would understand each other. I am certain they have asked pardon for their former behavior and we might even become friends, since time would

132

have canceled the difference in age. The bookshop! I never pardoned Her for having made me wait so long on that cursed afternoon. Deep inside, I always blamed Her for the vexation of being harassed and affronted by that band of urchins pretending to be intellectuals and revolutionaries when they were neither, as the future demonstrated: their names were never on book covers nor on the "Most Wanted" list of the police.

My practical reflections and their corollaries concerning Her destiny had begun in a climate of great sympathy but ended up making me feel distrustful and sour. The change must have been reflected on my face. Her expression had altered too. The tranquil silence that had accompanied the beginning of my thoughts about business had given way to an anxious muteness. I prolonged my wordlessness in order to stifle my irritation and think better. I forced myself to take in the whole of Her narrative and the new situation that had arisen; I went over the principal themes, making adjustments and readjustments, trying to weigh everything in an objective manner with maximum honesty toward myself and Her. Once more I managed to face the events as if I had nothing to do with the story. Only this time, what stood out was no longer the pathetic but the comical side of most of the situations. I recognize that the women in my life were all more intelligent than I, and, among them, Her position is prominent. However, they all took such a serious view of life that in the area of humor I come out indisputably ahead. I was a funny fellow as a lad, with success at school and in the German beer halls of old São Paulo. I changed markedly, but behind the severity imposed by business and personal relationships I retained a few traces of my old lightheartedness. Apparently I had bottled up a store of unused laughter, since from the time I was twenty I had been faced with situations that constrained me to austerity both at work and at home. My interior reserve of fun, never finding any chance to escape, had built up past the safety limit without my realizing it. Mentally summarizing the skeletal plot of Her story, I saw a virgin crawling out intact from beneath the superior, inferior, and middle members of a first man to be twice deflowered by a second in order to marry a third. The whole thing had such a similarity to the verbal games in vogue at my liceu or the idle conversations in the Rutli, City of Munich, and Franciscan bars, that I was transported back to my youth, and the floodgates of maturity were burst asunder. The result was a deluge of laughter that left me literally stretched out in my chair, shaken by interminable peals of mirth that threatened to choke me, sobbing to the point of convulsion from merriment. The attack must have lasted for some time since I didn't see Her get up. When I managed to compose myself a bit, dabbing my wet eyes with my pocket handkerchief, I saw Her standing in front of me, livid, trembling from head to toe. Still coughing, I squelched the desire to start laughing again and gasped a few words of apology for my rudeness. Her lividity changed to redness; her body stopped trembling; she stretched out her hands as if to strangle me and screamed two sentences that pierced through house, garden, and street.

"Paul Dior, you can go straight to hell with your good manners! Shove 'em up your ass, Dr. Polydoro!"

Before she said the last word I had time to observe that Her voice had changed: it had acquired a young tone, vulgar but crystal clear. My reaction was so instantaneous that I only realized what I had done when I saw, covering more than half her face, the reddish mark left by my hand. A thread of blood was oozing out of her left nostril and a stronger flow from her mouth. She shook her head to dispel the dizziness caused by the dry shock of the blow and fled.

Immediately I grew calm. I could hear Her voice talking on the phone and was worried at what she was saying. Naturally she was speaking with her cousin and I foresaw the rest: proven evidence of bodily harm from the Institute of Legal Medicine, a litigious divorce, complete victory, my family gloating and me deprived of more than half my fortune. But just then I was more worried about something else. I had just discovered Her and had lost Her in the same moment. I had never really loved Her and now it was too late. At bottom, I had always judged Her to be as artificial and well mannered as I. During our so-called happy period, I had made Her the super-butler of my court of servants and, when this period was over, I had thought of Her as an old domestic whose discharge was complicated by the employment laws. Even after hearing her long biography I hadn't really come to know Her, because she spoke in the voice she had adopted to please me long ago when she came to work in my office. Whether or not she said agreeable things, she had always remained the same and had only changed in the last seconds of that night when she insulted me. The instant she hurled the swearwords at me, that entirely new voice unveiled the existence of a Her different from the three I knew: my three Hers of work, comfort, and tedium—not to mention those of Dr. Bulhões. The new Her was the cousin's, potentially intact inside the others, repressing itself for me and repressed by me, the only

one that I could have truly loved. It was Her of the
Quarta Parada, a street girl with bad habits, vivid
tongue, and shrill voice, Her whom I had met seconds
before she pronounced the only intolerable swear-
word, my name, and left me forever, her teeth broken
from my blow. My only excuse is that I acted in legiti-
mate defense against the rabid jackal that leaped, not
out of Her mouth, but out of the depths of my childish hell, to torture me again.

Having been arrested in 1936 for protesting against the fascist Vargas regime, PAULO EMÍLIO SALES GOMES (1916–1977) escaped to Europe, where he studied film and began work on his now classic biography of the seminal French director Jean Vigo. Instrumental to Brazilian cinema as a professor, historian, and advocate, *P's Three Women* was Sales Gomes's only completed work of fiction. He was married to Brazilian author Lygia Fagundes Telles.

MARGARET A. NEVES has translated work by Jorge Amado, Antonio Torres, Moacyr Scliar, and Edgard T. Ribeiro.

SELECTED DALKEY ARCHIVE TITLES

PETROS ABATZOGLOU, *What Does Mrs. Freeman Want?*
MICHAL AJVAZ, *The Golden Age.*
The Other City.
PIERRE ALBERT-BIROT, *Grabinoulor.*
YUZ ALESHKOVSKY, *Kangaroo.*
FELIPE ALFAU, *Chromos.*
Locos.
JOÃO ALMINO, *The Book of Emotions.*
IVAN ÂNGELO, *The Celebration.*
The Tower of Glass.
DAVID ANTIN, *Talking.*
ANTÓNIO LOBO ANTUNES, *Knowledge of Hell.*
The Splendor of Portugal.
ALAIN ARIAS-MISSON, *Theatre of Incest.*
IFTIKHAR ARIF AND WAQAS KHWAJA, EDS.,
Modern Poetry of Pakistan.
JOHN ASHBERY AND JAMES SCHUYLER,
A Nest of Ninnies.
ROBERT ASHLEY, *Perfect Lives.*
GABRIELA AVIGUR-ROTEM, *Heatwave and Crazy Birds.*
HEIMRAD BÄCKER, *transcript.*
DJUNA BARNES, *Ladies Almanack.*
Ryder.
JOHN BARTH, *LETTERS.*
Sabbatical.
DONALD BARTHELME, *The King.*
Paradise.
SVETISLAV BASARA, *Chinese Letter.*
MIQUEL BAUÇÀ, *The Siege in the Room.*
RENÉ BELLETTO, *Dying.*
MAREK BIEŃCZYK, *Transparency.*
MARK BINELLI, *Sacco and Vanzetti Must Die!*
ANDREI BITOV, *Pushkin House.*
ANDREJ BLATNIK, *You Do Understand.*
LOUIS PAUL BOON, *Chapel Road.*
My Little War.
Summer in Termuren.
ROGER BOYLAN, *Killoyle.*
IGNÁCIO DE LOYOLA BRANDÃO,
Anonymous Celebrity.
The Good-Bye Angel.
Teeth under the Sun.
Zero.
BONNIE BREMSER, *Troia: Mexican Memoirs.*
CHRISTINE BROOKE-ROSE, *Amalgamemnon.*
BRIGID BROPHY, *In Transit.*
MEREDITH BROSNAN, *Mr. Dynamite.*
GERALD L. BRUNS, *Modern Poetry and the Idea of Language.*
EVGENY BUNIMOVICH AND J. KATES, EDS.,
Contemporary Russian Poetry: An Anthology.
GABRIELLE BURTON, *Heartbreak Hotel.*
MICHEL BUTOR, *Degrees.*
Mobile.
Portrait of the Artist as a Young Ape.
G. CABRERA INFANTE, *Infante's Inferno.*
Three Trapped Tigers.
JULIETA CAMPOS,
The Fear of Losing Eurydice.
ANNE CARSON, *Eros the Bittersweet.*
ORLY CASTEL-BLOOM, *Dolly City.*
CAMILO JOSÉ CELA, *Christ versus Arizona.*
The Family of Pascual Duarte.
The Hive.
LOUIS-FERDINAND CÉLINE, *Castle to Castle.*
Conversations with Professor Y.
London Bridge.

Normance.
North.
Rigadoon.
MARIE CHAIX, *The Laurels of Lake Constance.*
HUGO CHARTERIS, *The Tide Is Right.*
JEROME CHARYN, *The Tar Baby.*
ERIC CHEVILLARD, *Demolishing Nisard.*
LUIS CHITARRONI, *The No Variations.*
MARC CHOLODENKO, *Mordechai Schamz.*
JOSHUA COHEN, *Witz.*
EMILY HOLMES COLEMAN, *The Shutter of Snow.*
ROBERT COOVER, *A Night at the Movies.*
STANLEY CRAWFORD, *Log of the S.S. The Mrs Unguentine.*
Some Instructions to My Wife.
ROBERT CREELEY, *Collected Prose.*
RENÉ CREVEL, *Putting My Foot in It.*
RALPH CUSACK, *Cadenza.*
SUSAN DAITCH, *L.C.*
Storytown.
NICHOLAS DELBANCO, *The Count of Concord.*
Sherbrookes.
NIGEL DENNIS, *Cards of Identity.*
PETER DIMOCK, *A Short Rhetoric for Leaving the Family.*
ARIEL DORFMAN, *Konfidenz.*
COLEMAN DOWELL,
The Houses of Children.
Island People.
Too Much Flesh and Jabez.
ARKADII DRAGOMOSHCHENKO, *Dust.*
RIKKI DUCORNET, *The Complete Butcher's Tales.*
The Fountains of Neptune.
The Jade Cabinet.
The One Marvelous Thing.
Phosphor in Dreamland.
The Stain.
The Word "Desire."
WILLIAM EASTLAKE, *The Bamboo Bed.*
Castle Keep.
Lyric of the Circle Heart.
JEAN ECHENOZ, *Chopin's Move.*
STANLEY ELKIN, *A Bad Man.*
Boswell: A Modern Comedy.
Criers and Kibitzers, Kibitzers and Criers.
The Dick Gibson Show.
The Franchiser.
George Mills.
The Living End.
The MacGuffin.
The Magic Kingdom.
Mrs. Ted Bliss.
The Rabbi of Lud.
Van Gogh's Room at Arles.
FRANÇOIS EMMANUEL, *Invitation to a Voyage.*
ANNIE ERNAUX, *Cleaned Out.*
SALVADOR ESPRIU, *Ariadne in the Grotesque Labyrinth.*
LAUREN FAIRBANKS, *Muzzle Thyself.*
Sister Carrie.
LESLIE A. FIEDLER, *Love and Death in the American Novel.*
JUAN FILLOY, *Faction.*
Op Oloop.
ANDY FITCH, *Pop Poetics.*
GUSTAVE FLAUBERT, *Bouvard and Pécuchet.*
KASS FLEISHER, *Talking out of School.*

FOR A FULL LIST OF PUBLICATIONS, VISIT:
www.dalkeyarchive.com

[symbol]

SELECTED DALKEY ARCHIVE TITLES

FORD MADOX FORD,
The March of Literature.
JON FOSSE, *Aliss at the Fire.*
Melancholy.
MAX FRISCH, *I'm Not Stiller.*
Man in the Holocene.
CARLOS FUENTES, *Christopher Unborn.*
Distant Relations.
Terra Nostra.
Vlad.
Where the Air Is Clear.
TAKEHIKO FUKUNAGA, *Flowers of Grass.*
WILLIAM GADDIS, *J R.*
The Recognitions.
JANICE GALLOWAY, *Foreign Parts.*
The Trick Is to Keep Breathing.
WILLIAM H. GASS, *Cartesian Sonata*
and Other Novellas.
Finding a Form.
A Temple of Texts.
The Tunnel.
Willie Masters' Lonesome Wife.
GÉRARD GAVARRY, *Hoppla! 1 2 3.*
Making a Novel.
ETIENNE GILSON,
The Arts of the Beautiful.
Forms and Substances in the Arts.
C. S. GISCOMBE, *Giscome Road.*
Here.
Prairie Style.
DOUGLAS GLOVER, *Bad News of the Heart.*
The Enamoured Knight.
WITOLD GOMBROWICZ,
A Kind of Testament.
PAULO EMÍLIO SALES GOMES, *P's Three*
Women.
KAREN ELIZABETH GORDON, *The Red Shoes.*
GEORGI GOSPODINOV, *Natural Novel.*
JUAN GOYTISOLO, *Count Julian.*
Exiled from Almost Everywhere.
Juan the Landless.
Makbara.
Marks of Identity.
PATRICK GRAINVILLE, *The Cave of Heaven.*
HENRY GREEN, *Back.*
Blindness.
Concluding.
Doting.
Nothing.
JACK GREEN, *Fire the Bastards!*
JIŘÍ GRUŠA, *The Questionnaire.*
GABRIEL GUDDING,
Rhode Island Notebook.
MELA HARTWIG, *Am I a Redundant*
Human Being?
JOHN HAWKES, *The Passion Artist.*
Whistlejacket.
ELIZABETH HEIGHWAY, ED., *Contemporary*
Georgian Fiction.
ALEKSANDAR HEMON, ED.,
Best European Fiction.
AIDAN HIGGINS, *Balcony of Europe.*
A Bestiary.
Blind Man's Bluff
Bornholm Night-Ferry.
Darkling Plain: Texts for the Air.
Flotsam and Jetsam.
Langrishe, Go Down.
Scenes from a Receding Past.
Windy Arbours.
KEIZO HINO, *Isle of Dreams.*
KAZUSHI HOSAKA, *Plainsong.*

ALDOUS HUXLEY, *Antic Hay.*
Crome Yellow.
Point Counter Point.
Those Barren Leaves.
Time Must Have a Stop.
NAOYUKI II, *The Shadow of a Blue Cat.*
MIKHAIL IOSSEL AND JEFF PARKER, EDS.,
Amerika: Russian Writers View the
United States.
DRAGO JANČAR, *The Galley Slave.*
GERT JONKE, *The Distant Sound.*
Geometric Regional Novel.
Homage to Czerny.
The System of Vienna.
JACQUES JOUET, *Mountain R.*
Savage.
Upstaged.
CHARLES JULIET, *Conversations with*
Samuel Beckett and Bram van
Velde.
MIEKO KANAI, *The Word Book.*
YORAM KANIUK, *Life on Sandpaper.*
HUGH KENNER, *The Counterfeiters.*
Flaubert, Joyce and Beckett:
The Stoic Comedians.
Joyce's Voices.
DANILO KIŠ, *The Attic.*
Garden, Ashes.
The Lute and the Scars
Psalm 44.
A Tomb for Boris Davidovich.
ANITA KONKKA, *A Fool's Paradise.*
GEORGE KONRÁD, *The City Builder.*
TADEUSZ KONWICKI, *A Minor Apocalypse.*
The Polish Complex.
MENIS KOUMANDAREAS, *Koula.*
ELAINE KRAF, *The Princess of 72nd Street.*
JIM KRUSOE, *Iceland.*
AYŞE KULIN, *Farewell: A Mansion in*
Occupied Istanbul.
EWA KURYLUK, *Century 21.*
EMILIO LASCANO TEGUI, *On Elegance*
While Sleeping.
ERIC LAURRENT, *Do Not Touch.*
HERVÉ LE TELLIER, *The Sextine Chapel.*
A Thousand Pearls (for a Thousand
Pennies)
VIOLETTE LEDUC, *La Bâtarde.*
EDOUARD LEVÉ, *Autoportrait.*
Suicide.
MARIO LEVI, *Istanbul Was a Fairy Tale.*
SUZANNE JILL LEVINE, *The Subversive*
Scribe: Translating Latin
American Fiction.
DEBORAH LEVY, *Billy and Girl.*
Pillow Talk in Europe and Other
Places.
JOSÉ LEZAMA LIMA, *Paradiso.*
ROSA LIKSOM, *Dark Paradise.*
OSMAN LINS, *Avalovara.*
The Queen of the Prisons of Greece.
ALF MAC LOCHLAINN,
The Corpus in the Library.
Out of Focus.
RON LOEWINSOHN, *Magnetic Field(s).*
MINA LOY, *Stories and Essays of Mina Loy.*
BRIAN LYNCH, *The Winner of Sorrow.*
D. KEITH MANO, *Take Five.*
MICHELINE AHARONIAN MARCOM,
The Mirror in the Well.
BEN MARCUS,
The Age of Wire and String.

FOR A FULL LIST OF PUBLICATIONS, VISIT:
www.dalkeyarchive.com

SELECTED DALKEY ARCHIVE TITLES

WALLACE MARKFIELD,
Teitlebaum's Window.
To an Early Grave.
DAVID MARKSON, *Reader's Block.*
Springer's Progress.
Wittgenstein's Mistress.
CAROLE MASO, *AVA.*
LADISLAV MATEJKA AND KRYSTYNA
POMORSKA, EDS.,
Readings in Russian Poetics:
Formalist and Structuralist Views.
HARRY MATHEWS,
The Case of the Persevering Maltese:
Collected Essays.
Cigarettes.
The Conversions.
The Human Country: New and
Collected Stories.
The Journalist.
My Life in CIA.
Singular Pleasures.
The Sinking of the Odradek
Stadium.
Tlooth.
20 Lines a Day.
JOSEPH MCELROY,
Night Soul and Other Stories.
THOMAS MCGONIGLE,
Going to Patchogue.
ROBERT L. MCLAUGHLIN, ED., *Innovations:*
An Anthology of Modern &
Contemporary Fiction.
ABDELWAHAB MEDDEB, *Talismano.*
GERHARD MEIER, *Isle of the Dead.*
HERMAN MELVILLE, *The Confidence-Man.*
AMANDA MICHALOPOULOU, *I'd Like.*
STEVEN MILLHAUSER, *The Barnum Museum.*
In the Penny Arcade.
RALPH J. MILLS, JR., *Essays on Poetry.*
MOMUS, *The Book of Jokes.*
CHRISTINE MONTALBETTI, *The Origin of Man.*
Western.
OLIVE MOORE, *Spleen.*
NICHOLAS MOSLEY, *Accident.*
Assassins.
Catastrophe Practice.
Children of Darkness and Light.
Experience and Religion.
A Garden of Trees.
God's Hazard.
The Hesperides Tree.
Hopeful Monsters.
Imago Bird.
Impossible Object.
Inventing God.
Judith.
Look at the Dark.
Natalie Natalia.
Paradoxes of Peace.
Serpent.
Time at War.
The Uses of Slime Mould:
Essays of Four Decades.
WARREN MOTTE,
Fables of the Novel: French Fiction
since 1990.
Fiction Now: The French Novel in
the 21st Century.
Oulipo: A Primer of Potential
Literature.
GERALD MURNANE, *Barley Patch.*
Inland.

YVES NAVARRE, *Our Share of Time.*
Sweet Tooth.
DOROTHY NELSON, *In Night's City.*
Tar and Feathers.
ESHKOL NEVO, *Homesick.*
WILFRIDO D. NOLLEDO, *But for the Lovers.*
FLANN O'BRIEN, *At Swim-Two-Birds.*
At War.
The Best of Myles.
The Dalkey Archive.
Further Cuttings.
The Hard Life.
The Poor Mouth.
The Third Policeman.
CLAUDE OLLIER, *The Mise-en-Scène.*
Wert and the Life Without End.
GIOVANNI ORELLI, *Walaschek's Dream.*
PATRIK OUŘEDNÍK, *Europeana.*
The Opportune Moment, 1855.
BORIS PAHOR, *Necropolis.*
FERNANDO DEL PASO, *News from the Empire.*
Palinuro of Mexico.
ROBERT PINGET, *The Inquisitory.*
Mahu or The Material.
Trio.
A. G. PORTA, *The No World Concerto.*
MANUEL PUIG, *Betrayed by Rita Hayworth.*
The Buenos Aires Affair.
Heartbreak Tango.
RAYMOND QUENEAU, *The Last Days.*
Odile.
Pierrot Mon Ami.
Saint Glinglin.
ANN QUIN, *Berg.*
Passages.
Three.
Tripticks.
ISHMAEL REED, *The Free-Lance Pallbearers.*
The Last Days of Louisiana Red.
Ishmael Reed: The Plays.
Juice!
Reckless Eyeballing.
The Terrible Threes.
The Terrible Twos.
Yellow Back Radio Broke-Down.
JASIA REICHARDT, *15 Journeys Warsaw*
to London.
NOËLLE REVAZ, *With the Animals.*
JOÃO UBALDO RIBEIRO, *House of the*
Fortunate Buddhas.
JEAN RICARDOU, *Place Names.*
RAINER MARIA RILKE, *The Notebooks of*
Malte Laurids Brigge.
JULIÁN RÍOS, *The House of Ulysses.*
Larva: A Midsummer Night's Babel.
Poundemonium.
Procession of Shadows.
AUGUSTO ROA BASTOS, *I the Supreme.*
DANIËL ROBBERECHTS, *Arriving in Avignon.*
JEAN ROLIN, *The Explosion of the*
Radiator Hose.
OLIVIER ROLIN, *Hotel Crystal.*
ALIX CLEO ROUBAUD, *Alix's Journal.*
JACQUES ROUBAUD, *The Form of a*
City Changes Faster, Alas, Than
the Human Heart.
The Great Fire of London.
Hortense in Exile.
Hortense Is Abducted.
The Loop.
Mathematics:
The Plurality of Worlds of Lewis.